ALSO BY TAMARA JERÉE

Novels

The Fall That Saved Us

Novellas

A Wolf Steps in Blood (Spring 2024)

A VISION OF MOONLIGHT

& OTHER STORIES

TAMARA JERÉE

WATER SIGN BOOKS

CONTENTS

INTRODUCTION

All but one of the stories collected for this book were written between 2019 and 2021, several of them when I had the luxury and pressure of the workshop setting. Like many authors, I have the writing-stories-since-I-could-hold-a-pencil backstory, but 2019 was the year I found my voice and began writing with an intention I'd never had before. Fighting to defend my artistic influences and interests in academia taught me an invaluable lesson in what I wanted my work to be.

These years also saw me complete grad school and grapple with all the pressures that life places on artists. I took a detour into the video games industry and came out on the other side with an even stronger sense of what I needed in my creative life.

Reflecting on the start of my writing career and finally having my debut novel in hand inspired me to revisit these stories. I wanted to present them as a collection, putting two anthologized stories side-by-side with the others from online magazines. I wanted to hold each one up and look at what themes I was circling and how they've developed in my current work.

Two stories—"To Devour a Star" and "When You Find a Dragon"—are a gift from my younger self, the nerd who couldn't get enough stories of kids going on magical adventures with dragons. "When You Find a Dragon, Name Them for Me" is my first story that was ever accepted for publication and the first short story that, after a year of struggling with the form, ever *clicked*. "On Lore," an all-vibes little flash piece, was the second to be accepted, but the dragon lore I'd created in that first story wouldn't let me go. A year later, I wrote "In Case You're the One to Devour a Star," a very loosely connected prequel where I wanted to explore how people started feeding stories to dragons in the first place. But really, it was another opportunity to write sapphics in love, something I was scared of for too long.

Of the ten stories in this collection, several are flash fiction, a form I swiftly took to. As a dabbler in poetry, I love the ability to work closely with an image when it strikes and focus on the mood of a fragile turning point. With the occasional short story, I've had the thought of writing something longer in the setting, but the flash pieces, more than the others, feel especially *done*. They arrive fully formed like dreams or nightmares, and for a precious hour or two, I feel like I'm channeling or communing with something beyond myself.

"Despair, Divided," a flash piece written in 2021 and published in 2022, brings us to where my work is today—romance where outcasts and outsiders find the one who *gets them* and, in the process, find a way to healing.

As always, thank you, reader, for joining me on this journey.

CONTENT NOTES

"A Serpent for Each Year" has themes of mourning parental death.

"Not Death nor the Storm" contains death rituals and mourning of a grandparent.

"Despair, Divided" is a fade-to-black sex scene.

"In Case You're the One to Devour a Star" mentions pregnancy, birth, and terminal illness.

"In Our Season" features a crisis hotline and themes of seasonal depression.

"The Future in Salt Water" contains consensual body transformation.

"A Vision of Moonlight" contains body transformation, death, and drug use.

"For Want of Sisterhood" contains poisoning, sexual content, and death.

A SERPENT FOR EACH YEAR

OUR RELATIONSHIP IS ALMOST a year old when I ask Nal why she is covered in snakes. I thought it might have been rude to ask before, to look too long at the undulating mass of scales that obscures much of her body. Just as a snake slithers away and I glimpse a cheek, an elbow, an eye, another is there in its place as if to spare her the cruelty of being seen. She says her mother put them on her one by one, a serpent for each year Nal survived, but now her mother is gone, and the snakes she has now are the only ones she'll ever have. The snakes twist across her body, agitated, as if they too know that the mother is no more, that her protection will fade as they age.

I tell her that, in my homeland, parents do not give their children snakes. We celebrate birthdays with sweets and parties.

"But does that last?" Nal asks me. "Will those sweets be there to mourn with you when your parents are gone?"

Nal tries to give her snakes peace by naming them variations on her mother's name: Lizzie, Beth, Eliza, Liz, Eli, Liza. When she inevitably exhausts the conventional and resorts to Zabeth, I do not critique. Although I have never lost someone, I tell myself that we all have our ways of mourning, ways of existing with the emptiness.

Zabeth is the snake who never calms. Zabeth nests on Nal's head, is ouroboros around her neck, winds up her arm in memory of Asclepius' staff, joins another snake on her leg to form a faux caduceus. "Where is

Zabeth?" I tease her when she wakes from a nap, when she emerges from a bath, after she has been bent over her work for hours. Sometimes if we spend enough time gently prodding her masses of snakes in search of Zabeth, they'll tickle her, and she'll giggle. I miss hearing her laugh.

Our relationship is barely two years old when the first snake dies. Nal rolls over to snooze her alarm, and there's the still snake, twisted all wrong and belly up, on her pillow. I am scared it is Zabeth. I have never lost someone I cared about before. I don't know how to lose someone I care about even after watching Nal do it. I don't know what kind of person I will become if I lose someone I care about. My parents fed me sugar to mark the passage of time, and I do not know bitterness, do not know what it's like to feel dozens of rough, shedding bodies—all on the cusp of great change—grating against my own. I am afraid of feeling. And so I lie there in the near-dark with my selfish fear, and only when Nal stirs, as if to wake, do I look to see who it is on the pillow.

NOT DEATH NOR THE STORM

T HE WITCH OFFERS NIS the elder skull. Nis shows her how to call the threshold of death.

From the peak of the ossuary, Nis visualizes the jagged tower of bones as a knife that will slice the hurricane. They imagine themself as the willowy pines that bend easily under the force of nature. That is Nis with the dead—accepting their power and anger but never breaking. Nis times their meditation so that it will coincide with the start of the hurricane and they can trance through its power.

The dead wake them as they are slipping under. They so rarely all speak at once, but now they fill the ossuary with the insistent rattle of bones, portending something other than the storm.

In silence, light only the black
candles. The red, save for after.
When lighting the censer, many

will see the silhouette of the
door. It is not for you to open
yet.
- from *The Eleven Verses of
Death,* Caretaker Lith Imn

Imagine what we will be able
to see when freed from skin
and our eyes are ever open.
- excerpt from caretaker
correspondences

They meet when the witch is unconscious. The wards around the tower
have struck her down just as the wind begins to wild. Already the air is
heavy with water and thick to breathe. Prone, the witch curls protectively
around a pale shape that calls to Nis. A spirit seeks home. Nis hovers closer.
Within the witch's hood, her face is sharp-featured, but her skin is the
same warm brown as Nis's own. They have the sudden and confusing urge
to reach out and trace the sharp bridge of her nose, but the witch smells
of florals and astringent herbs—scents that disturb and haunt the dead.
Nis hopes it won't cling to their robes. Strapped to the witch's back is a
lumpy gray sack that Nis is certain is filled with skeletal remains. Clutched
protectively in her hands is the skull, Nis realizes. The wind tugs at the
bell of the witch's sleeve, whipping it back to reveal an inked pentacle on

the back of her hand. The mere sight of it curls Nis's lips in a hiss. Final confirmation that the wards were true. Indeed, they've snared a witch.

Briefly, Nis wonders if it's a trap of some kind, if the witch knew they would be drawn out of the tower when they sensed the bones. They dismiss it. The witch is the foolish one if she did not expect the wards, the storm. She must have traveled from the lands in the north where they do not know the fury of the coastal season.

Nis takes the bones first, setting them carefully inside the tower. Trap or not, these bones belong to this land.

Safe within the candlelit glow of the ossuary, Nis peers out at the witch, still unconscious in the pine needles and grass. If she weren't a witch—and if Nis hadn't sworn themself to a life of isolation in service of the dead—perhaps they might attempt to name this dawning feeling.

The first droplets of rain darken the steps. Nis hopes they will not regret dragging the witch out of the storm. Holding their breath, they find the offending packet of herbs on a cord around the witch's neck and toss it into the wind.

The witch reveals her name. Witches, unlike other people, do not introduce themselves or merely *give* their names. They *reveal* them.

Its power courses through the dark of the ossuary. Nis, trained to see threads of power, seizes it. They could string the witch up like an occult puppet, could bind her in her own name as with invisible rope. Against the common wisdom of the Catacombs—*never suffer a witch lest she torment the dead*—Nis does not.

The witch and the caretaker stare across the gloom of the ossuary, altar candles burning low between them.

Nis tests the name, pulls the power taught. The witch holds her chin up. Defiance or daring, Nis can't tell. They let the power slacken and dissipate.

"Why reveal your name to an enemy?" Nis asks.

"To prove to you that we are not."

> The body is the key. Bone is portal. The skull, intention. Cast the circle with what remains.
> - from *The Eleven Verses of Death*, Lith Imn

> I have dreams of reaching into myself and withdrawing my own bones, clean and sun-bleached.
> - excerpt from a caretaker's unsent letter

Shadows sharpen the bones that crowd the walls. Nis follows the witch as she walks the perimeter of the central chamber, studying their arrangement. The witch cranes her head back, gazing up to where a tower of thigh bones are lost to the darkness of the upper tower. At first, Nis worries that they will have to warn her away from touching the remains, but the witch keeps a respectful distance that seems at least partially born of uncertainty. Nis has never seen anyone look at the interior of a bone sanctuary with such unease, but they remind themself that this is the first time the witch would have encountered the traditional deathways.

"The coven mother denied my grandmother's request that her body be treated according to her tradition. She said you all commit blood sacrifices in the name of the dead," says the witch.

"We sacrifice no one but ourselves," Nis answers, their voice echoing back to them. "At Mirthe, we learn that witches gain their power by stealing it from the dead. That you put them in the ground so they can never cross over and find peace."

The witch draws her gaze away from the bones and back to Nis. "We derive our magic from our ancestors, yes. But we keep them close to us so that they might walk by our sides and teach us, so that we might still dance with them. We have no afterlife to ferry them to. There is only this life."

Nis doesn't understand. They have sacrificed this life for the afterlife. They cannot fathom a world without it, cannot fathom a world where the dead stay to dance with the living. There is no peace without crossing.

"Then why have you sought the Bone Sanctuary of Minam bu Mir?" Nis asks.

"My grandmother married into our coven, the only outsider among us. This land of red clay is hers. She wanted to return to be with her family," says the witch.

Nis aches to smooth their hand over the elder's skull, to listen for the echoes of her life and understand who would leave her land for the bitter cold north and its strange magic. Nis has only ever known one life path. So many like them, the ones who will not grow up to be woman or man, become caretakers. It is not ordained, but enough people expect it that it seems so. That expectation and the desire to live—even briefly—among others like themself had driven Nis to the Catacombs of Mirthe and, finally, to Minam bu Mir, where they would live out the rest of their days alone.

To be a caretaker meant they would never want for company. That's what the senior caretakers in the Catacombs of Mirthe taught the young ones. The serenity of solitude would fulfil them. Nis had never known loneliness, they realize, because they have lived with it so long that they have become numb to it—or else it has numbed them. They don't have the space to understand which, only that they are grateful for this storm and this witch and this blessed death.

"Your blood is also of this land," Nis tells the witch over a plain meal of broth and crusty bread. The smell of bright foods unsettles the dead, and rich meals could rouse caretakers from the meditative state they work to maintain. Nis has not considered their food in years but can tell by the look on the witch's face that she was expecting something much different after her long travels. They has nothing else to offer, so they ask, "Did your grandmother lead you home?"

The witch pushes back her hood and combs her fingers through her dark braids. Their silver ornaments glint in the candlelight. "She was concerned with her death in a way many in my coven are not. She left a box with specific instructions—a map to Minam bu Mir, precise directions about when to exhume her bones, descriptions of landmarks and customs. People thought she was becoming fragile in her old age. I'd always liked her stories. I thought I'd listened to her well and knew the way."

"Home calls to us all. We must return."

The witch frowns. "I have only come to fulfill the wishes of someone I loved. I will return to my coven—if the coven mother will have me back after my defiance."

Rain lashes the windows high above. Wind still rattles the heavy doors in their frame. For as long as the storm lasts, they will not be alone. There is tension in its reassurance.

"We must accept our own," Nis says, trying to convey understanding. They consciously try to disentangle their wants from the witch, try to remember how to converse outside ceremony. "How strong could a coven be that casts out its own?"

"I hope the mother feels that way," says the witch. She stares pensively into her bowl of broth. "They say the dirt to the south is red because it's absorbed bad magic. I thought, as I walked, that it looked vibrant. Just like my grandmother said. I'd like to see more of this place, but I have risked so much by leaving at all."

"Take the land with you when you go," Nis says. They go to the cupboard and return with a small cup that they offer to the witch. "I made it from the red clay."

It is a sturdy, rustic piece, but the witch takes it as if it's spun from the most delicate glass. Their fingertips brush, and Nis jerks their hand back at the contact. They can't remember the last time they touched another's bare skin. Bones are all that have existed of bodies for so long.

The witch notices, and her smile is slow and shy. Nis can't meet her gaze, so they clear the table.

Dip your hands into the threads
of magic. Trace your fingers

over the curve of the skull to
bathe it in power. If the spirit
has not yet turned their eye to
you, now they will.
- from *The Eleven Verses of
Death*, Caretaker Lith Imn

I have dreams of building
myself into the ossuary walls.
- words for a torn page

When the doors cease their rattle, Nis takes the witch out to see the eye of the storm. She's hesitant at first.

"Won't it come back?" she asks, lingering just inside the doorway.

"It will, but we have a few moments," says Nis.

The world has been blown apart. Pine needles stick to the bone-pale tower. Branches hang heavy and drenched. An old tree, one that could no longer bend, is snapped in two. The green is darker, richer from the rain. The wet earth is molten red. On the air, minerals and damp. A circle of serene blue sky looks down on them, its edges jagged with swirling clouds.

The witch steps out as if into a new world, staring up at the sky with her mouth open. She reaches for Nis as if to balance herself, and Nis lets their hand be taken. There is no edict against contact with the living, but Nis still feels as if something has been broken.

Only after they're safely inside and the storm has redoubled does the witch notice her missing herbs.

"I blessed them for safe travels," she says. "They would not have harmed you."

"But they would have made the bones restless."

Nis has only been possessed once outside of ritual. The bones of someone who had died alone in the wild had been delivered to them. During their life, Nis discovered, the person had suffered much psychic torment. As soon as Nis lay their hands on the bones, the spirit had sensed an openness in them and poured into their body. Nis had lost time in the spirit's turbulent mind, and when they managed to separate from them, they had collapsed into a deep, week-long sleep on the stairs of the ossuary. It was an extreme case with an already-unstable spirit, but disturbing bones often brought bad energy onto a caretaker.

"I can give you something to make up for it, a protective talisman," says Nis.

Their chest constricts when the witch initially balks at the skull of the catacomb rat. They hasten to explain. They do not carry disease and they are not pests. The rats that live in the Catacombs of Mirthe have the most developed spiritual sense of any nonhuman and are given to young initiates to help them sharpen their intuition into intention.

"Their bones are sacred and treated with care," says Nis. "If you listen, they will warn you of danger."

Again, the witch accepts the offering with both hands. "Please forgive me. You've given me another meaningful gift, more than I could repay."

The ache in their chest eases. "I would be remiss not to make up for discarding your herbs out of hand."

"No, no," says the witch. "It is ultimately a blessing. Thank you."

Caretakers are not often thanked. Mourners and the dead have so much more to occupy their minds, after all. Like skin, like body heat, Nis struggles to process it.

The spirit will flood into you. They will want the door because it is freedom, but it will rebuff them. First, they must unburden the woes of this life to pass into the after. Through agony, you are a conduit for peace.
- from *The Eleven Verses of Death*, Caretaker Lith Imn

I've lost the ability to discern dreams from nightmares from memories.
- excerpt from a caretaker's love letter

"Can I watch you guide my grandmother into the afterlife?" the witch asks.

"Most do not want to witness the possession," says Nis, sweeping incense ash from the altar in preparation. "The dead must shed their pain and worldly attachments to cross over, and even the most fulfilled, happy spirit can twist a caretaker. There are parts of every life, secrets, that it might hurt the living to know. Even to other caretakers, witnessing someone in the throes of possession can be unpleasant."

The witch steps up to the altar, cradling the elder's skull in her hands. Nis is struck by the sight. Perhaps if she wore black robes and bore the ritual scarification that marks their cheeks, Nis might mistake her for a fellow caretaker.

"I'm not afraid," says the witch.

"Of what?" Nis almost snaps. An emotion prickles that they haven't felt in ages, and they wrestle to name it. If they let it run wild, it would ruin their focus. "Of possession, of pain, of death?"

"I'm not afraid of you, Nis."

No one has ever told them that. Among the people, caretakers are respected. After all, everyone's death rests in their hands. Respect, however, does not mean that their people look upon them warmly. So many families, when they bring their dead to the ossuary, can maintain only fleeting glances. That Mirthe dictates the caretakers' isolation to protect their spiritual attunement means that they will never be any less mysterious to the people they serve.

"May I?" the witch asks, hands outstretched.

Nis doesn't know what she's asking for but nods before even considering it. The witch places the skull carefully upon the altar before stepping up to Nis and studying their face. Her gaze is so open, and Nis is so unused to eye contact, that they struggle to hold it. They remember how, in their days as an initiate, they struggled to subdue the wildest spirits. Now, Nis feels that they must apply the same learned principles to their own heart. The witch runs her hands over the stubble of Nis's scalp, pushing back their hood as she goes. Nis shivers even though, now hours into the storm, the air is warm and damp. The witch trails her fingertips down the nape of Nis's neck and brings her hands to cup their face, brushing her thumbs first over the row of scars along their cheekbones and then over the dusting of black pigment on their eyelids. Nis breathes through the touch the same way they have learned to breathe through pain.

"Does it hurt to be touched?" asks the witch.

It does—in a way that Nis doesn't want to explain. "No," they reply, breaking.

The spirit unburdens.

Nis has never needed to consider the consequences of breaking the isolation tenant. Not that they could have shoved the witch back out into the storm. But they could have offered food and retired to their room at the tower peak. They could have abstained from sharing conversation and gifts. They could have declined to share the ritual.

Nis has never struggled to hold a spirit before, especially not one so gentle. The sense of severing is the strongest, the cutting ties from home. It manifests as sharp pain in Nis's chest, and the grounding glow of the candles and smoke of the incense are lost to them. They find mingled regret and hope. Embarrassment diluted by indignation. The burden of carrying the old ways in silence, lest they be ridiculed. Smothering half of the self.

The correct words feel distant. Nis gropes through their memory for what they should do next. They are not in their body, not psychically, but they can feel the pain of it.

Someone is pulling at the threads around them, sweeping up the tatters and stitching closed the wounds. The spirit's pain is shunted away as if it has found another path. Nis gasps for breath and remembers the words to move beyond.

"I see you. I will remember," Nis says and means it.

As if they have surfaced from dark and oppressive depths, the candlelight returns. To Nis, it seems so bright. They find the edges of themself and realize their body is on the hard floor. The witch kneels beside them, forehead wrinkled with concern. When their eyes meet, the threads cradling Nis cling a little less desperately.

Nis senses the spirit's attention turn before passing over the threshold. They know her relief, her thanks—not only for the unburdening but for Nis's kindness towards her descendant. The spirit has possessed them, and the spirit knows the thing Nis themself doesn't want to acknowledge most.

When the pressure of the spirit departs, Nis attempts to take a full breath and feels as if a smaller storm rages inside their chest. The witch rests a hand there and breathes for them both.

When a spirit departs, it is normal to feel hollow for a time. Know that possession is the most sacred rite. Without caretakers, there would be no peace. If the hollowness lingers beyond a moon, return to Mirthe to undergo ritual cleansing by an elder caretaker.
- from *The Eleven Verses of Death*, Caretaker Lith Imn

How does one hold an entire
life and then return to one so
empty?
- question scrawled in the
margins of a copy of *The Eleven
Verses*

The world outside is dark when the storm leaves them.

"Is it always so bad?" asks the witch. Nis knows she means the ritual and not the storm.

Nis lights the final red candle. They will burn through the night and purify any lingering energy. In the morning, Nis will find a place to arrange the bones with the others along the ossuary walls.

In the morning, the witch will depart.

"I'm not often so careless," Nis answers, studying the burn of a candle.

"You weren't careless. You were giving. Open. Such a big offering could hurt anyone. It's a wonder you're not wearier."

"We train years for this. It should not have gone this way tonight." Nis realizes that they feel embarrassed, that other caretakers might find it shameful to have needed help from an outsider, especially a witch. Nis wouldn't have been in this position if the witch hadn't come—but they also wouldn't have discovered what they have. Nis sets aside their bruised ego and faces the witch. "There are so few willing to do this work that it is necessary to work alone, to rely only on oneself. The way you pulled the threads was delicate yet supportive. Thank you."

The tension in her expression eases. "You're welcome. When I saw your pain, I acted first and only considered later how it might've been improper of me. I'm relieved that it wasn't. Our magic traditions may be different—and I hope I'm not too forward in suggesting this—but I might still be of assistance. So you wouldn't have to shoulder so much alone."

Both are silent for a moment. "But your coven. You said you intend to return if they would have you back. And the senior caretakers at Mirthe would—" Nis doesn't know what they'd do, what they'd say. The witch is one of their own by blood, but a witch still.

"The coven has been my world for my entire life. I love it." She steps nearer, voice turning wistful. "But I also want to experience this place I've only known in stories, to walk the paths my grandmother did."

"People would be suspicious of you. You couldn't hide your marked hand forever."

"But perhaps it would be different if you were with me. The people trust you."

Nis goes to sit on the stairs and rests their face in their hands for a moment. They aren't used to feeling, and it exhausts them. They feel shaken apart, unruly, chaotic. "What you suggest isn't done. People's trust in the caretakers is not what you imagine. It is respect, but it is not warmth."

The witch hovers near. "I'm sorry. I've been presumptuous. I've scared you."

"I'm not scared," Nis says, realizing it is a lie as they say it. *It doesn't hurt.*

The ossuary is too quiet without the wind and rain. The witch sits beside them on the stairs, careful to leave space between them. They watch the candles burn, and Nis feels the storm gathering in their chest again. Nis became a caretaker to find solace with kindred souls. A younger Nis thought they wouldn't mind the isolation their duty required. They had spent their entire life in the company of the living and still felt lonely.

Then death and a storm drove a witch to their doors.

They need to recenter. Need to meditate. Need to refocus on the days ahead—days that will inevitably run together as they always have. They knows they will begin to mark time by this day, will every year anticipate the hurricane season bringing her back to them.

They have known hundreds of lifetimes, feel old beyond their years in some ways, and yet here is this giddy hope they don't want to tamp down.

"My room is upstairs if you—" Nis doesn't know how to ask. "I don't want to be alone."

The witch looks at them. Half her face is lit by the red glow of the candles. She waits.

Nis stumbles through an explanation of themself, discovering that they both have different words for the same thing. Eventually, the two arrive at an understanding. Neither wants sexual intimacy but would enjoy physical affection. Both exhale nervous giggles of relief.

Nis offers their hand, and they ascend the spiral stairs together.

The red candles burn themselves out sometime in the pre-dawn morning. Nis wakes at the subtle shift of energy.

The bed is too narrow for them both and the air is still sticky from the storm, but Nis is at peace if not comfortable. The witch sleeps open-mouthed and not quite snoring, her back nestled into the curve of Nis's body. They prop themself up on an elbow to better study her face, mentally composing the letter they will send to Mirthe. Dawn will come for them, but Nis wants to suspend this moment, hold it the way time in the afterlife moves but does not advance.

DESPAIR, DIVIDED

ARCANE GRIPS MY HORN implants, maintaining eye contact as ve guides me down to the bed. I'm flattered that ve's taken on a corporeal form just for me. Arcane says ve knows how humans couple (*couple*—ve is, in fact, an old old god) and asks if that's what I'd like from this experience. (Ve calls it an *experience* too.) I say I want whatever ve will give someone like me—someone tossed out of their home in the upper city and forced to make a life underground. Someone who knows the shitty metal in their body will one day give them cancer but collects mods like trophies anyway. I'm afraid to ask why ve's chosen me—afraid to ruin a good thing or else acknowledge a bad one while it still feels good.

In this form, Arcane has a head, and ve tilts it at my words. "So we are both fallen, in our own ways."

"What were you the god of?" I ask.

Arcane traces my mods as ve thinks: hand pausing at the patches of black scales on my shoulders, the spines down my back. Ve presses a finger into my mouth and finds steel-plated fangs. "Loss, despair," ve answers distractedly.

Ver words settle heavy and cold. "As in…you brought despair?"

"I removed the despair of others into myself."

I relax. There is so much despair in Lower Providence. "You mean you took those feelings away?"

"Yes."

"Was that…" I don't know how to talk to a god. I didn't know they existed until recently. I lick my lips and catch my tongue on the point of a fang, something I haven't done in years. My mouth tastes like metal as I say, "It sounds like a nice thing to do for people."

Take my despair. Take it. The plea leaps to my mind, unbidden.

At that, Arcane finally returns my gaze—if it could be considered that. Ve has voids where ver eyes should be, but somehow I know ve's regarding me more closely. I realize, perhaps, that ve heard my thoughts as a prayer. If so, it was my first.

"I can give you bodily pleasure," ve says, ver tone haunted by something like regret. "That will have to suffice."

"Yeah, 'course," I say. I lick my lips bloody.

How do you make love to a god of despair? I wonder, even as it happens. There are things one can't say. I couldn't beg for ver to fill me, as ve is empty—the fissures in ver gray skin revealing the nothingness within. I couldn't breathe against ver neck and whisper how much I wanted ver body—for it was not a body but a hollow and temporary vessel. Ve seems aware of this—in ver first tentative touches, in ver questioning glances. Ve seems braced for a look that would betray my repulsion of ver form, then softens when it never appears.

"I want you to pin me down," I say.

Ve does, and they weigh nothing and everything. They are the condensed hopelessness in my chest. They are the numbness that follows tears. I gasp at the sensation. Ve releases me as if worried I'm hurt. I hold them—as if my mortal body could do anything against a force so deep and old. Ve kisses me. My tongue quests into ver mouth and it too is empty. When ve withdraws, I realize I'm crying.

"I warned you of this," ve says.

I huff and swipe at my eyes. I shove a strap-on harness at ver. Ve seems baffled by the neon dildo.

"Fuck me," I say, throat still tight.

"Only if you are—happy." Ve stumbles into the last word.

"Are you happy?" I counter.

Ve laughs with ver mouth closed.

In another moment, perhaps it might be comical: Arcane—with ver gray skin and lank black hair and void eyes—sporting a jutting pink dildo. But the anticipation of fucking a god would make anyone breathless.

Arcane doesn't leave when we're done. Ve looms by my bedside, studying me with ver eyeless gaze. I decide to give ver a pass on ver lack of etiquette. Ve is old. Maybe ve's new to this hooking up thing.

"Do you...often have sex with humans?" I ask.

"You're the only one."

That makes me sit up. "Why me?"

"You remind me of someone from the old days. Someone I was close to."

"Are they not around anymore?"

Arcane returns to the bed, hovering just over the sheets. "How is your despair?" ve asks.

"You mean to ask how I'm feeling," I correct.

"Yes." Ve traces from my horn to my chin. If an eyeless gaze can be tender, this is it. "How are you feeling?"

In the void I see my own emptiness reflected back. I find a grim triumph in the observation: here, at my lowest, a god looks upon me. Even in the dark, I can touch the divine.

My smile bares my fangs. Arcane's answer is my second prayer, a conjuring of what could be—for me, for us both.

IN CASE YOU'RE THE ONE TO DEVOUR A STAR

I'M UPFRONT AT OUR first meeting in the courtyard. If Lilist is going to reject me because of my shortened lifespan—and she has all the right to, as the others I've met before her—I'd rather she do it sooner. Before I begin imagining what the future could be.

"I'm not really first-mother material," I say, looking down into my tea. Has she already noticed the starry scent of dragon feathers clinging to my robes? Does she think the tremble in my hands is due to nerves or the fatigue of harnessing fire all day?

She places her cup back into its saucer. This is it, I think, but she smiles and says, "What a relief."

Women who are destined to be first mothers want to make families with other aristocrats. Occasionally, one will decide they want the comfortable pace of life that comes with marrying a craftswoman from the flatlands. "No one wants to make a family with a fire keeper," I say because in my months of seeking a partner, this is the resounding impression I've internalized.

I have loved life in the monastery. I was born there and never wanted any other life. For most of us, the fire is all the warmth we need; the companionship with fellow fire keepers all the relationships we'd want. Among us, there is no strangeness in looking skyward and dreaming of outer worlds.

My hands are clattering the teacup against its saucer. It's nerves now, I'm sure. I set it on the table between us. She's not staring at the cup or my hands. Her gaze is locked on mine.

"I might want to, Iris."

I have talked to wild dragons and seen them eclipse the moon. I have caught the fire of their breath in my hands and taken its power into myself. Yet suddenly I feel fear speeding my heart as I face this woman who could have anything else but claims she wants to have a family with a fire keeper. People in Vel do not remarry. Choosing a fire keeper as a partner means spending most of one's marriage always knowing that time is against them; that one day very soon, they'll be alone.

She reaches across the table and strokes the swath of scar tissue on the back of my hand. "It's an old injury," I tell her automatically, as if her touch was a question. "From when I was young. The first time I tried to hold a dragon's breath. My control slipped."

Her voice is soft when she speaks, as if anything louder could aggravate my old wound. "Is it common? Burns like this?"

"All of us have a story. Most of us, more than one." A pause. Perhaps Lilist, a poet, is more inclined than most to listen to the stories of someone like me. "Am I the first fire keeper you've ever talked to?"

"There aren't many of you compared to us. Most don't choose your life."

From the mouths of some, this may have been an insult. With her, it's an observation. She keeps stroking my scar, and I watch the trace of her fingers.

"I think your work is fascinating—what I know of it, anyway," she says next, and I'm so hypnotized by the delicate pressure of her fingertips that I almost miss what she's said.

Two first mothers glide by our table—I can tell they're firsts by their embroidered silk capes and measured strides, the crystals braided into their long hair. They glimpse Lilist's hand on mine, blink, bend their heads towards each other. I have not left the monastery in weeks, not since the last rejection. I wonder what I look like to them in my muted colors, with my long but singed hair. Foolish of you to grow it out, my teacher had admonished. You can throw off your cloak if it catches fire, but long hair is an unnecessary hazard. The short hair, though—it gives us away as fire keepers when we come down from the mountain. That's what the first woman I talked to said.

Lilist watches the two retreating first mothers, then fully grasps my hand. "Let's walk," she says.

I cling to her like she is living fire.

Lilist and I marry against the advice of her parents and sister, when I have, at best, five years left to live.

"What will you do when I'm gone?" I ask her when we're secure in the dark of our room one night. Lilist's bed is piled with beaded and embroidered cushions and wide enough to fit two more people. If not for her weight against me, I would have felt insecure in its opulence. "People say life feels colder after their fire keeper dies." Her head is pillowed on my chest, and I know she must hear how my heart races.

I cannot see Lilist's face. Eventually she says, "Then you will just have to show me how to tend the fires as you do."

She finds my hand again like at that first meeting, and I offer to share the final piece of my life with her.

When I travel to the monastery for the first time after our marriage, I bring Lilist with me. She has traded her silk gown and velvet cape for wool and furs at my advice, and only a jeweled broach, hairpin, and rings betray her status. The wind in the mountains is harsh without the shelter of the monastery's walls and the heat of dragon breath. Thankfully, though, there is a well-traveled path. When I tell her of it, Lilist insists on bringing her horses, saying that I might be fit enough to scale mountains on my own strength but that she is not used to the exertion. So we ride.

"Are you more used to riding dragons?" Lilist asks as we begin our journey, and I can't help my laugh.

"Is that what you all think down there in the city?"

"Fire keepers do have a reputation for being..."

"Daredevil fanatics?" I suggest.

I intended it as a joke, but she says, "I'm sorry. There are so many rumors. I should know better than to put stock in any of it."

"If any of us could tame and ride a dragon, we'd have mighty spirits indeed. What would stop any of us from going off to the stars with them, visiting other worlds?"

Lilist falls quiet in that thoughtful way she has. When she speaks again, she says, "Tell me if I am out of line for asking, if these are secrets of your order, but— Where do the dragons come from? Why are they here?"

These are the questions the highest of our order have asked since the first contact with dragons. I tell Lilist this, that we haven't yet learned their tongue but can interpret the vague outline of their will through sharing fire. They say they have come from another star system. They say their star went out, devoured by one of their kind, and their world became intolerably cold. We cannot yet interpret from their account why the devourer did this.

"The most concrete thing we have learned from them is the star map," I finish.

Nightfall brings a clear sky. I locate the halfway alcove and we make camp, watering and feeding the horses and ourselves. With the mundane tasks done, I withdraw the flask of fire I keep next to my heart. Lilist still marvels at how the flame dances without fuel, how its container is merely warm to the touch.

"Do you have a bit of parchment?" I ask, because of course she, a poet, would have thought to bring parchment on a trip into the mountains.

She nods and fetches a roll from her things. I spread it flat on the stone.

"The star map looks best at night," I explain. "It's beautiful. I want to show you."

I have never worked fire outside of the company of the other fire keepers, much less in front of someone uninitiated into our world of heat and smoke. Most people, still wary of the dragons and the ones who associate with them, do not want to witness one of us working fire, but Lilist's eyes are bright in the darkness as she watches me unstop the flask and inhale the flames.

I have missed the burn in my throat, my mouth, my lungs. I am careful to avoid looking too closely at Lilist as I sink into the ritual. Although I do this for her, I cannot allow myself to think of her. A trace of anxiety can ignite a flare, set off an eruption that would swallow us all in flame, and so I imagine that I am alone while I brew the fire. Despite the wind, I'm sweating. Suddenly, I need to shrug out of my cloak. It falls heavy at my feet, and I gaze past Lilist up into the stars and let the dragon's memory become my own. I exhale the smoke, as my training has disciplined me, and let the fire inside grow. Many apprentices, at this stage, will expel the fire before it can brew its magic, but I know the point at which my body will blister and ash, and I've learned to banish the fear of that possibility.

Out of the corner of my eye, I notice that Lilist has drawn her furs tighter around her, is staring at me with something I don't have the space to name if I'm going to control the fire. The horses are whinnying, snorting, pawing at the ground. Lilist thinks to go to them and soothe them.

Spark. That is the way we're all taught to recognize when the fire has brewed the magic to its peak. Ironic, when you have an entire inferno coursing through you, that you'd recognize anything so nuanced as a spark, but it makes intuitive sense. I feel it as a prickle along my spine. I seize it and visualize its shape. I kneel to the paper and blow a tame lick of flame. The parchment catches, crisps, and blackens as the flames dance over its surface. I exhale smoke once more and breathe the fire back into the flask. By the time I've wiped my brow and gulped down the clear air, the parchment has fully ashed and the map has set. I beckon Lilist over to see.

Some of the ash has crystalized into a spattering of starry flecks burned into the stone at our feet. Through them, a gossamer trail charts a course. I point up at our stars and show Lilist where they are on the scale of this map, where the tiny galaxy spirals out to represent stars we can't see with our own eyes. I show her the course the dragons took through the eternal night, and she sits back and looks at me and then at the map again.

"I feel so small," she says. "Everything feels so small."

I don't expect her to say this. "For us, the dragons make us feel connected to the potential of all the other worlds they've visited on their way to us. Their fire grounds us in our bodies and to the earth in the way nothing else has ever done or could do. None of us would ever give up the pain of fire, because it brings so many gifts," I say. I need her to see how beautiful this is, why I do not hate my scars, why the wildest among us devote ourselves to this life. Sometimes one is born with a spark to draw the terrifying unknown to themselves and confront it and at least gain contentment by knowing the depth of the mystery.

"I understand, Iris," she says in the too-fast way of someone who doesn't truly understand. She strokes the scar on my hand as she looks back to the star map.

Her gesture is kind, but for once, it doesn't reassure me. Maybe that's because of the sudden exhaustion that comes with working fire, or maybe it's the memory of a lifetime defending our study to outsiders, but I feel an old weariness that threatens this precious moment. I grip the flask of fire with my free hand. An unconscious gesture. A comforting one.

Lilist knows it well by now. She squeezes my hand, and I have her full attention. "It's beautiful, Iris," she says. "Your work is beautiful. Thank you for sharing this with me."

The weariness abates, and it comforts me that, soon, Lilist will see the monastery. When she does, I know she'll understand.

None of us in my lifetime have ever brought partners to the monastery. It is not forbidden, but it is rare; rare enough for one of us to marry, and rarer still for us to want to return in the company of an outsider. Uncertain of the etiquette, I sent a letter ahead of us, introducing Lilist and asking for my old teacher's blessing. Her response was curt, in keeping with her usual manner, and confirmed that she wouldn't stop someone from scaling the mountain if it was in their heart to do so.

"She didn't say yes," Lilist had pointed out, pacing with the letter in hand. "I wouldn't want to be an imposition."

"It's a yes."

"How do you know?"

"I know her."

And so we'd gone. Certain that everyone would adore Lilist as much as I, I hadn't worried—not until the familiar shape of the monastery's buildings came into view.

Those walking the upper paths have already seen us approaching on Lilist's great mares, and a small gathering, all drab cloaks and close-cropped hair, welcomes us. In the time I've been gone for the wedding, some of the youngest already have new burns or have earned their own flasks of fire strung around their necks. I embrace each person there, and if they have their own fire, it warms my chest as we touch. When I reach my old teacher, she smiles her usual tight, controlled smile and remarks that my hair is growing ever longer.

In the silence that follows, I turn back to Lilist, still sitting high on her horse. Silhouetted against the sun, she appears more imposing than I ever remember her being. I go to her to help her down, and she moves as if to hold her skirts out of the way, then remembers herself. Except for this trip, I've never seen Lilist in trousers.

An entirely different kind of heat, the uncomfortable kind, rises in my face as I turn to introduce my wife to the people who, in any way that matters, have been my only family. They kiss her cheeks and compliment her pretty jewels, glittering things that ceased to catch my attention the longer I spent in Vel. Suddenly, I see her again as I saw her that first day, as they must see her—a cautious aristocrat too pampered by life to see its mysteries.

My teacher does not kiss her cheeks as the others have done, only looks at me and says, "She must be cleansed with smoke before she comes any farther," then retreats in the direction of the sanctuary, leaving me standing amid the silent stares of my peers.

The ceremonial smoke clings to Lilist's hair and clothes, and I love the smell on her. With ash smeared across the bridge of her nose, she looks like one of us, a new initiate. I show her the monastery grounds, carefully avoiding the sanctuary and my teacher and the dragon who sleeps there during the day. Everyone is eager to tell her the history of not only our modest quarters but the entire mountain, and the youngest of us clamor after her, asking for stories of Vel. I stand back and admire how they dote on her.

The night will be clear again, and I suggest that we stay up and watch the dragon's lunar flight. The night-lights are brightest at the top of our mountain, and on a full moon like tonight, the lunar eclipse brought on by the span of the dragon's wings is even more stunning. So we huddle in the courtyard with the others in the too-cold night on the iced-over snow. Lilist shivers against me, and we all hush when we sense midnight. The ground shakes. I know how to brace for it but, in my familiarity, I have neglected to warn Lilist. I steady her before the next shake and whisper an apology. My teacher appears from the dark mouth of the sanctuary, striding easily towards us over the trembling ground. She acknowledges us all with a nod, and we wait.

Lilist grips my hand when the dragon's head emerges from the cover of the sanctuary. Each step makes the mountain below us tremble, but we are staring up, lost in the dewy glisten of the dragon's silver feathers and the opal glint of their horns. Their great head lowers to us and they turn one colorless eye to Lilist, who watches, steadily, in return. The dragon's mouth parts, and Lilist stumbles back against me in alarm, but only a warm smoky breath washes over us, insulating against the chill for a few precious seconds. The others try to suppress giggles and fail as Lilist sags against me. My teacher smiles a real smile.

From their perch atop the rocky point of the sanctuary, the dragon summons the currents that will buoy them into the night sky. They circle above us, a low, fast shadow. As they circle higher, we can track their progress by the trail of stars disappearing and reappearing, renewed and brighter than before. When they circle low again to confront the moon's light, I hear Lilist breathe in and keep her breath until the moon is freed from shadow of wings and the dragon's feathers carry the faint glow of the moontouched. Now, I think, she understands.

I might have thought my living space modest before, but it appears severely austere after spending time in Lilist's rooms in Vel. We squeeze together on my narrow bed, and I tell her stories of what we've gleaned from the dragons, breathing out smoke images to illustrate the strange things the dragons have told us of: that the celestial lights we call stars are far-flung suns much like ours, that planets of gas and ice and eternal storms also circle our sun, that in the cold dark of space, collapsed stars become light-eating voids.

"That's terrifying," says Lilist, curling closer to me. "Are you sure the dragons aren't speaking in metaphor?"

"It's real. I've witnessed it through fire."

"The same fire that shortens your life," she says. Not accusatory, just fact. "Our bodies were never meant to hold power as untamable as fire, and you pay dearly for it."

She's quiet for a moment, and though I know our relationship has passed the point where many others would have shunned us for our heretical beliefs, I still feel the prickle of worry that comes with divulging draconic wisdom to an outsider. In Vel, most tolerate our presence when we come down from the mountain to trade for goods, but when one of our order long ago tried to share what we'd learned of starfire and the properties of dragon feathers, they were violently driven from the city for daring to—in the Velians' words—"proselytize the teachings of offworlders." Now, we are careful what we say about our lives and the structure of the universe.

"I understand," Lilist begins slowly, "why you would trade your time for such precious truths."

"Just as a poet seeks truth, if I understand your craft correctly."

This draws a smile from her.

She combs the tangles out of my hair, smooths the kinks with flower oils, and braids them into intricate swirls across my scalp. When I marvel at myself in her mirror, she says that perhaps my teacher will stop scolding me if it's held back.

"Maybe," I say and thank her.

"Do you think," she starts tentatively, "I could talk to the dragon as you do?" When I am too surprised to respond, she hurries on to say, "It was just so beautiful. Tonight. And it's not as if daughters of families like mine even have the chance to consider becoming fire keepers."

I repeat to her the first lesson my teacher taught me. "To meet a dragon for the first time requires a gift. Take some time to consider what of value you might give."

On the last day of her visit to the monastery, Lilist settles on a gift. It is not any of her jewels but a piece of parchment I have seen her laboring over far into the night.

Under the watchful eye of my teacher, we enter the sanctuary together, the warmth of the space immediately banishing the outside chill that had settled into us on our way. A great pyre lit by dragon's breath burns in the center of the cavernous space, and in the shadows, the dragon looks up as if seeing the sky through the rock above us, white eyes radiant with the light of lost stars.

Lilist slips the rolled parchment from her sleeve and bows before the dragon. They blink as if the greeting has jolted them from their starward trance. With the patient slowness of one who has seen ages, they bend their head so that they no longer tower over Lilist and can meet her gaze as an equal.

"I am a poet, and I have written a song for you," she says. The dragon shifts, settling their head upon clawed feet. They wait.

Lilist sings, and it is not a song for noble halls or ballrooms. The words are in our tongue but not organized in our way. Rather than telling a story, she weaves a suggestion among us, an emotion like longing. She sings as if breathless, and as the song unravels, I never hear her inhale. The song grows like a fire given all the fuel it has ever hungered for, and I think of wings, although she does not mention them. I feel the possibility of weightlessness, the threat of the vast dark.

Lilist is shaking when she's done, and she offers the parchment that holds her words. The dragon considers it, then whispers its breath over one corner of it, setting it alight. Lilist doesn't startle at the fire and waits fearlessly as the dragon opens its fanged mouth to take her words and swallow them whole. They press their nose into Lilist's hand and close their eyes, as one does when letting a drink warm them from the inside on a winter night.

Lilist otherwise holds still but turns her head so that I can see her smile. The restrained joy of it is a precious thing, and I also fight my expression into something befitting the weight of the moment. My old teacher hums her approval, the closest she ever comes to praise. The dragon has accepted both Lilist and her offering, and she now has a new home here with my peers and I in the sky.

Because of Lilist, we begin to feed the dragon our stories. Whenever I come down from the monastery to visit her in Vel, she has a roll of parchment for me to take back to the dragon who likes her stories best. She encourages other poets to write to the dragon so that our stories might not be lost, so that Vel may travel the cosmos in the belly of a dragon. Soon, I am making my way back up the mountain with satchels overflowing with parchment, and people are making pilgrimages to visit the dragons who were once so feared.

We birth a child who is preternaturally warm. Lilist says this is because the child grew in my belly and learned to hold fire before they knew anything else. That first winter after their birth, Lilist will not let them go, holding selfishly to their warmth. There is fear in that grasp, but I do not name it aloud. I understand how looming death would make one cling to life. I make the dangerous winter climbs to the mountain alone.

My years are burning down to embers when we finally return to the courtyard where we first met. It is summer now, and despite the heat, Lilist still clings to the child. We sit among the verdant plants and guess at what names the child might take for themself when they're old enough to choose, but Lilist quiets when the reality that I won't see that moment with her comes drifting back. Time beyond the next moon has gradually stopped existing for us. Lilist is always so careful not to talk about years; holidays—anything that marks the passage of time—turn her somber. I can no longer clear the smoke from my lungs, and I cough with every other breath. Heat has made my tongue unable to enjoy the rich foods we used to savor together. I haven't told her this. I eat and drink and describe, based on memory, how wonderful it is. I am sure to smile across the table at her.

"Will you show me how to make the star map?" she asks.

I look at her, and she has so much fire in her eyes for someone who has never harnessed dragon's breath in her body. "You can't," I say. I do not tell her she could learn. There are things even I am still afraid of. I have loved this life, but I do not know if I want Lilist to follow me into it. I don't want to wonder how the fire will deteriorate her body after I'm gone. "And I have shown you the star map before. You remember it?"

She sits back. Watches the baby in her arms. "I couldn't forget," she says.

"When our bodies are ashed, the dragons take us up into the stars," I say, and I do not know why I've said it, only that it feels suddenly urgent. On their wings, we are dusted among nebulae; raw elements to be folded into the formation of new worlds.

"Won't you ask them to leave some of you here on earth with me?"

I cough and say, "For you, the dragons would do anything."

I take the flask of fire from around my neck and breathe without its weight against my chest for the first time since it was bestowed on me. At my death, this fire will be returned to the dragon and they will have my memories, just as I have held theirs. I have loved this life. Years ago, I wouldn't have thought it would mean so much to me for someone outside the monastery—someone other than the dragon—to remember it too.

I study the dance of the flame and fold its flask into Lilist's free hand. She looks at her fist as if it's a star map, as if it's something that needs discerning. When she returns her gaze to me, I breathe another unburdened breath and tell her, "When the time comes, I want it to be you who returns my fire to the dragon. They'll see my life—our love—and know your wish to keep some of me here with you."

When You Find a Dragon, Name Them for Me

I SEE THE DRAGON feather first, but when I record our progress for the day, I will write that Nihla was the one to discover the first hopeful sign. I will give her that kindness, a gift that will only matter if we find the dragon and don't die in the middle of the wastes. If my manuscript survives as long as those of the greatest poets in my family, I will not only be giving her a kindness but bestowing even greater honor upon her. Few ever touch a dragon's feather, whether it is still attached to the dragon or not.

The feather is only as long as her forearm and radiantly black. She bends to it with reverence, the loose end of her headscarf falling to conceal her face as she does. The first peaceful silence of the journey falls between us. I move to her slowly as if the feather is a fragile thing that will dissolve if I stir the air. We stare at it, shiny despite the gray sky; lush in defiance of the wilting around us. Nihla strokes it. The clouds are swirling again, but we don't feel any wind here on the ground.

She eyes the feather now with a glint in her eyes that makes me uncomfortable. "Is your command of language enough to capture my discovery? Or should I suggest some words for you?"

I clench my teeth but manage to reply mildly, "My Book was passed to me by my second mother. She wouldn't have done so if I couldn't uphold the poetic decree to set words beautifully and faithfully."

At that, Nihla turns away from me. She holds the feather in front of her like a torch. I briefly wonder if draconologists possess their own magics, secret methods of divining direction from abandoned pieces of a body. Then I remember her disrespect. I've never known even the greatest draconologist to wield magic that equaled the abilities of a novice poet. Even when I was young, I could trace a finger across the page of an elder poet's book and glimpse histories as hazy afterimages. I could record and set my small everyday experiences in simple phrases by the time I was able to write with a mundane quill. Now, I could set entire days in close detail so that experienced poets could relive the past in mental projections. Now, I could project the histories recorded in my Book into other minds. Into dragons' minds. That's why I was chosen for this expedition in addition to three others. Three others who we've buried along the way, including the geomancer. This is why Nihla and I are lost now. I swear we've been circling the same stinking wasteland for days now.

I noticed the illusory stretch of the land a few hours in—the way big landmarks like the scattered trees and rare boulders kept away from us, the way the mud didn't keep the trail of Nihla's footprints—and was embarrassed how, in my exhaustion, I'd been unquestioningly following Nihla. She might have been chosen for the expedition based on her knowledge of draconic custom, language, and habitat, but she obviously knew nothing of the way deep magic could twist a land whose draconic protection was fading.

The mud of the geomancer's grave still stained our hems as we fought over what we should do next. I wanted to return home to Vel to find another who could guide us on our journey. Nihla had seen it as an opportunity to mock me for cowardice. I thought I was being pragmatic. We'd die wandering the wastes if we didn't know where we were going. The terrain changed every day. Sometimes we'd fall asleep beneath one of the old great trees only to wake by a putrid lake.

Then Nihla explained why we'd only had one geomancer to begin with. Vel couldn't part with another if the city were to survive and not be swept off into some void of deep magic as Adisa, the dragon guardian of Vel, aged and slipped into the afterlife. This was yet another instance, she'd said, that proved my immaturity. I was young and inexperienced. I'd never live up to my family's great name.

I run my fingers over my bag, finding the intricate patterns of my greatmother's tooled leather. I find a leaf there and trace it again and again. I have not seen a green thing in weeks. We have ventured so deep into the Far that we've abandoned our maps at the bottoms of our bags.

Nihla stomps the gravel. I follow. And so we are back to our uneasy silence. With no talk to pass the time, I feel I have seemingly infinite time to worry—and there's an infinite number of things to worry about now.

My first mother is a watchmaker because she says it puts her worry to use. Like everyone in Vel now, she worries over how much time is left. She used to count dried beans or the kinky strands of her hair, anything to take her mind off of my second mother's illness. Making the watches is the closest she can come to ever controlling or understanding time, and so she turns the gears. When I left, we hadn't eaten at our table for months because it was always scattered with toothy metal circles. I imagine her now in the kitchen, pushing her magnifying goggles up on her head when she hears my second mother turn over in her sleep. Going to my second mother's room because I am not there to help her. I am out in the wilds searching for Vel's dragon savior with Nihla who hates me.

We finally settle in a rocky outcropping amidst a stretch of flat marshland. I feel like I haven't slept since the geomancer died. Nihla and I have taken turns keeping watch which means little sleep for either of us. Watching for what exactly, I don't know, but before we lost the rest of our company, the one thing they were confident about was the unpredictability of deep magic. This desolate journey was easier when there were more of us to watch, more sleep to be had, the illusion of safety in numbers.

Nihla is watching the gray landscape, her back to me, perched neatly upon one of the driest uppermost rocks. Despite all the time spent out here, she still bothers with her little cleaning rituals: removing the mud or dust from her boots with that little brush she keeps in the side pocket of her pack, folding unworn clothes into neat squares, washing her brown blemishless face with those little potions that were all the rage at home. Back when we were comfortable and secure in our knowing, before our collective memory was endangered.

Adisa, guardian of our memories and the only dragon to ever watch over Vel, had grown weak and started forgetting the history and stories of our people in their old age. Consequently, children started to sometimes forget who their parents were and leaders forgot who they led and some people left for their daily work only to wander aimlessly.

I take out my Book to write as I always do when we stop to rest. It's never fully daylight out here in this part of the Far, but there's enough light through the constant clouds that I can see what I'm doing. My pen hovers over the page, and when nothing comes, I worry I am having a moment of forgetting. We are so far from Adisa after all. So I start with that wondering. I try to recall stories of our people travelling far without our dragon, and there are none. Or if they exist, I have forgotten them. I do not get stuck in that worry. I remember my first mother and try to keep my hands moving. I record in detail how Nihla found the feather. I embellish it a bit so that she seems more wise and less like a jerk. On the other side of the page, I record the discovery with all the tangled relief and desperation that I truly feel.

I flip between the two versions. It is our duty as poets to keep the dragons fed with our stories. I do not want to imagine feeding Adisa the more truthful second one. They are already so sick, and I know this thing would be bitter and drying on the tongue. If we do find the new dragon we came out here to search for, how could I entice it to return to our land with us if my Book is filled with angry, hopeless words?

I glance up at Nihla to make sure she's not watching. I don't want my ill second mother, our land's Great Poet, to know what I am about to do, but I am only paranoid. Nihla knows nothing about poetic teachings.

I put my hand to the more triumphant version, the one where, after losing many companions and wandering lost for days, we are reinvigorated with a symbol of hope. Nihla is a hero. I infuse the words with the intention needed to set them, and for a blink, my Book emits the most light I have seen all day. This story curls around my wrist one letter at a time, following the order of my quill strokes and stinging as it goes. The curving trail of the last words—*Nihla, triumphant*—burns itself onto the back of my hand. Words should not hurt. When I was young, the setting tickled until I got used to it. But it never hurt. I shake my hand as if it were the recent victim of a stinging insect, as if I can shake off the wrong words and the pain. I've never been self-conscious of the writing inked across my body. Even as a young poet, layers of disciplined script have blocked out sections of my brown skin in black stripes and rings. We are patterned like the great cats, my second mother says. I wear my ink with pride, but the ink of this story—this one itches like the beginings of an infection trapped under the skin. I tell myself I haven't lied. I shut the book hastily, and it falls closed with a thud. The other story, my truth, will fade within a day.

"Why don't you take first watch?" Nihla calls down. When we first set out, she used to complain about the occasional flashes of light from my Book as I set stories. Now she has already oiled and rebraided her hair, twisted her sleeping scarf over the fresh rows, and put out her bedroll on the flattest part of the rock to settle down.

Again, I am too tired to bother with my hair. The twists my first mother did for me are now frizzy, too dry. Maybe we'd be better off if Nihla put as much care into our mission as she did into her hair. Maybe then we would not have wasted time on illusions. I breathe and try to let the thought go. My second mother would never complain about her companions. Nihla is wrong to doubt my skills, but I am still not the poet my mother is. If I can't accomplish what she could, we will die and be forgotten. All of Vel will die, and as they do, they will wonder who failed them. So that I do not cry, I scratch the back of my hand and do as Nihla suggested. I watch.

The way ahead is ringed with mountains. We never get closer to them, which means we are very far from the dragons who might nest near their peaks. Nihla deigns to let me hold the feather as we start towards them again.

"It's either a tail feather from a very young dragon or a spinal feather from a middle-aged dragon. Middle age is about five hundred—"

"Yes, I know," I cut her off. My wrist is red from where I scratched it in my sleep. The back of my hand feels like it's starting to burn, and I hope the lack of sleep is only making me imagine that.

"We'd be very lucky to find a dragon of that age. Vel would be safe for centuries to come." She pauses, and I know something unpleasant is coming. "Do you think your craft is advanced enough to convince it to follow us home and hold our memories?"

"I wasn't chosen for this journey only because of my lineage."

"But it did sway the council's decision, I'm sure."

The burning itch seems to intensify at this. I rip the hem of my right sleeve and wrap my hand and wrist with the cloth. Nihla keeps walking ahead. "I am trying my best to honor my second mother's teachings and uphold my family's craft," I say. I've already gotten foul water in my boots once out here and so keep my eyes on the ground, but if Nihla persists in interrogating my worthiness, I will keep inventing insults that I will then have to bite back.

Were the other draconologists so busy doing important things, like keeping Adisa alive, that she was the only one they could spare? How competent of a draconologist is she if all she's managed to track down in days is a single feather? Could she even tell the difference between a dragon's spine and one of its teeth?

We are still early in our daily walk when Nihla suddenly stops. I am fussing with the bandage over my hand and almost run into her.

"What? Need to stop and wipe the mud off your shoes?" I grumble.

She turns and smiles, not at all like herself. "I meant to tell you how that last story you told to the children was perfectly delivered. Every word beautifully projected," she says.

"What...story?" I ask.

"The one about the poet and the moth."

I know this story. I know it very well, but I've never told it to Nihla. It is a story for young poets just learning to write.

"I wasn't telling a story," I say.

"Perhaps that's your problem. I'd lose my spirits too if I walked through this gray nothing and didn't have song or story. We must hold our joy close in these times."

Nihla's face hasn't changed—other than the fact that she is smiling for once—but I see a flicker of my second mother, Vel's greatest living poet, in the knowing curve of her lips. Remember the smile she'd given me before I set off. Her wish that, when I found a dragon who could be nourished by Vel's memories, that I name them after her.

"I understand now," I tell her.

She gives me a long look as if remembering something. Then says, "I'm going to miss you, sweet girl."

When her presence leaves, I know that Adisa now holds all her memories. I think about the intricacies of death ceremony and custom, how her body will be wreathed in sacred dragon flame, because it is easier than thinking about the loss itself. I hope my first mother was there to hold her before she died. I hope she did not strain her soul to come say goodbye to me. I think of my first mother sitting alone in silence but for all those ticking clocks and watches. The kind of grief that might break me down will have to wait until we return to Vel. My mother has urged me to have joy.

Nihla's face is Nihla's again. "What did you say?" she asks me as if she was only distracted by a pretty trinket in the marketplace. Then she looks at her shoes, the way the mud is sucking at them.

"I have a story I think you'll like."

In the time it takes me to tell the story about the moth, we are suddenly at the foot of the mountains, and my childhood feels oddly close. I've found the memory of the first time I held my poet's pen, a sleek brown feather gifted to my second mother by Adisa themself. I kept it on my bedside table and couldn't take my gaze off it for the entire night. Despite the lack of sleep, I was energized during my recitations and studies the next day. The feather has lost its luster and lush out in the Far, but as long as the warmth of the story lingers, I can feel the newness of this old gift.

"Finally," Nihla sighs. She does not remark on how the mountains which have seemed days away for weeks suddenly rise steep before us.

We can finally feel the wind again, and the sky is clearer here, peeking blue through white clouds. I tap a beat into the small drum that hangs from my belt, letting my hands settle into a rhythm that summons the next story. I drum through the bite of the lie clamped around my wrist. I want so badly to ignore it.

Other than the one-way communication of story, Nihla and I do not talk on our climb. Eventually, the path becomes so treacherous that I'm forced to concentrate solely on my footing. We often slip off our packs and press ourselves between high and narrow rock. Small animals scamper here, and when Nihla speaks, it is to voice her jealously at how easily they travel. My wrist aches from slinging my pack on and off and sometimes climbing when the strip of path disappears. I am trying not to favor it, but I do not keep up with Nihla's pace.

"Give me your hand," she calls down to me from a precarious perch.

I shake my head and press my forehead to the rock. The wind has whipped up again, and tears sting my eyes. My hand feels numb as if the lie around my wrist is choking off my blood.

Nihla curses, and it hurts in a way words haven't hurt me before. My chest tightens at the sound. I am still squeezing my eyes shut, so I don't notice when she stretches down to grasp me. Her grip tightens around my wrist, the bad one, and I cry out and slip. Nihla curses again and clamps down on me. I want to yell at her to let go. My body is suddenly a storm of pain. I do not remember that we are on a cliffside, that the only thing keeping me from tumbling to my death is her.

I am screaming when my back meets solid rock. Nihla is saying something to me, her voice rising as well. I do not know how long it takes the pain to subside. I cradle my hand to my chest and rock like a scared child.

"Your words are rotting!" Nihla cries. It's the first thing I understand. She stares at me like I might infect her with something, wavering between fear and concern. She's pointing at my hand, and I make myself look at it. The bandage, ripped in the rescue, is gone. Eager to deny what was happening, I haven't looked at my hand and wrist since I covered them. Now the skin around the words is black and festering like an untreated open wound.

Seeing it now, I cry.

"What's going on?" Nihla demands. She moves away from me.

I curl against the rock. "I only meant to help," I say to the wind stinging my cheeks, to the mountain, to Nihla.

"Tell me what you did. I've never seen a poet's words rot on their body."

I wipe my eyes, I breathe, and I tell her. I tell her about the record in my Book, the one I wrongly twisted to brightness. "I only wanted to make sure that when we found a dragon our stories could nourish it. Why would anyone want to eat bitter stories of a dying, desperate people?" Nihla doesn't say anything, and I add, "I was scared. I was scared and now—you're right. I've endangered everyone."

She won't look at me. "What happens now? Can we keep going?" I can hear the real questions behind the ones she asks. *Is there any reason to try? Will we die? Our people die?*

"I'll fix it," I say.

In a place where the mountain curves in against itself, we settle for the night. There's not enough space to put out our bedrolls properly, and Nihla and I share a blanket against the mountain wind. The rations of flatbread, bean paste, dry fruit, and nuts are low. We finished the last of our water before settling down for the night. We need to cross a mountain stream tomorrow.

Nihla's pack is still heavier than mine despite the low rations. I can hear the weight in the way it settles against the rock when she puts it aside. Probably extra jars of hair oil, knowing her. She notices me eyeing her pack with a frown. I think I might say something when she speaks first.

"You think I'm frivolous," she says in the whistling wind and the darkness, and I think I've heard her wrong. When I don't reply, she turns her head to me and continues, "I'm trying to remind myself that there's something besides fear and survival. Trying to remind myself to be tender with my body after putting it through this forced march every day."

I blink at her, let my mouth hang open for a moment as I wait for a reply to process.

"When we're not stuck on the side of a mountain, let me retwist your hair. I've got some flower oil left."

"Thank you," I say, struck by the way my resentment dissolves. I want to say more, but I don't know how to be vulnerable with her yet.

I comfort Nihla into sleep with stories, but my wrist keeps me awake. I slip from under the blanket and weigh my end down with my pack so that the wind doesn't take it. Nihla wrinkles her face and clutches the blanket. "I'm sorry," I whisper to her sleeping face. I take my book and pen and creep into one of the narrow breaks in the stone. I hope it is enough to shield any potential light from waking Nihla.

The Nihla I started this journey with would have wanted to throw me off the mountainside for what I've jeopardized. Now she is so tired and travel-worn, she's willing to believe I can turn my lies into hope. *I'm so sorry, mother*, I pray. I don't know if I'm still connected to Adisa so deep in the Far and especially after what I've done, but I hope even my weak apology reaches her.

My Book's pages reek of mold. I have not written in it since setting that mistaken story. Wedged deep in the rock, I open the Book to a random page and brace its heft against the opposite wall with my infected hand. I can barely see with the clouds crowding the moon, but that's no matter. Even in the dark, my off hand can inscribe words clearly enough to seize the magic in the Book. The feather of the pen feels suddenly too light in my hand. I am not an elemental caster like some in Vel, but I know just enough to cause destruction, and that's all I need.

I weave the elemental power with my words, inscribing the symbol for fire across the page. The Book grows warm, then hot. I tuck the pen safely in the hip pouch of my belt and watch the flames curl and blacken the edges of the Book's pages. I resist pulling my hands from the flames and dropping the Book. Fire licks the festering words on my hand and wrist and flares with the excitement of an animal who has sniffed out a trail. Blood floods my mouth, and I realize that I've bitten deep into my cheeks as I try to hold my agony down in my throat. My eyes burn with the purging light, and that's when I smell the burning flesh. Fire blazes for my face, and I let the Book drop and duck towards the entrance. One step back. Two. I can't look away from how the Book is curling in like a rapidly withering leaf, its innards ashing.

I cannot feel my hand anymore. It hasn't blistered as one would expect with natural fire. The words are gone. My skin is unmarked and smooth. But I cannot move it or feel it as if it had been cut from me years ago. I push back my sleeve with my other hand and see the absence of markings on my arm. No stripes. No rings. Despite my clothes, I feel naked. Part of me ripped away.

I cannot remember why I am clinging to a mountainside and huddled beneath a blanket with—with...

The woman next to me blinks her eyes into the haze of sunrise. The wind whips the floral scent of her hair into my face. She stares at my unmarked hand atop the blanket and seems to understand something.

"Nihla," I say because I have remembered her name.

She nods, but her face crumples with confusion. She puts her hand to her throat. "The dragon," she says as if this is the first time she's tried the words. Her voice is scratchy as if with sickness.

I show her what ashes remain of my Book, the ones the wind hasn't swept away in the night. She screams and shakes me, suddenly oblivious to how close we are to falling to our deaths.

"The only way to erase the lie, to stop the spread," I explain when she lets me speak.

She points to her head, and her eyes glisten with tears. "I'm already forgetting!" she exclaims.

I've severed the last connection we had to Vel, to Adisa, our language, and our collective memories. I don't know how much time we have until we forget the reason we came here and who we are.

"You were right," I say. I try to explain the molding Book, how the story would spread like a blight over our histories as it had done to the rest of my Book. I couldn't give a dragon what I'd written, but if we found a dragon soon enough, I could give them what I did remember, the stories ingrained in all poets before we're allowed to leave Vel. I try to hold that *if*. "I'm sorry," I say again. For the first time in my life, my words aren't enough.

We climb. I recite stories aloud to keep them centered. The moth who created the world and the first Book made from its wings. The geomancers born of earthquakes. The day the dragons arrived from the stars and helped us remember what we'd buried with our dead. I remember the images, but sometimes I stumble over the language to convey them. We've adopted so much of the draconic tongue for the old stories, and with the connection to Adisa lost, these words are fading fastest. Nihla has stopped speaking at all, and I wonder if it is because she has nothing to say to me or because she has forgotten all her words.

Nihla spreads the last of the bean paste on my flatbread because I haven't gotten used to doing things with only one hand. I smile at her in thanks, and she tries to smile back. I pray to my second mother again, repeating her name over and over in my head like a chant to channel a spell. I remember her wish to name the dragon after her.

It rains when we slow down for the day. The light hasn't set yet, but we are tired from our scant rations and lack of water. Nihla opens her mouth to the sky, the gesture a mix of childish whimsy and true desperation. I watch her and then follow suit to stop myself from choking on a sob. We stand like that for a moment, catching the spare drops of water the sky allows us. Suddenly, Nihla's hand grips my shoulder, then slips down to hold the hand that can't feel. I'm confused at first, but she tugs me towards something in the mud. Excitement animates Nihla's face out of the haze of forgetting. She drops to the ground and places her hand in a print in the earth. Her face hovers just over the mud like a geomancer divining a harvest. And there, the softening, rain-filled print of a dragon's foot. In the gathering shadows ahead, I make out a deeper darkness set into the rock, the jagged edges of an unnatural tunnel. Nihla nods. She knows the signs. I wonder if she has been listing them to herself to keep them anchored just as I have been reciting the old stories. We make it inside just as the storm settles into its rage. The rain beating the ground outside is a wall of sound at our backs. We stumble forward into the silence. My heart beats hard. Nihla squeezes my hand, and I hear so many words in her touch.

Darkness around us moves and shifts. I can hear it scraping along the rock. The upward burst of flame from the dragon's mouth illuminates the cave, and as the initial onslaught of heat and light dissipates, blossoms of magic flame remain suspended in the air. When the burn of light across my eyes relents, I see the owner of the feather we found, the black dragon. Nihla has lost her words, but she knows how to bow to the dragon. They tilt their head to her, and she immediately goes for the black feather in her pack and holds it out to the dragon as if returning a lost heirloom. She points to it, then to her heart, bows again. The angular face of the dragon turns to me, their dark eyes piercing in the light of the flaming flowers. I reach for the crest of the dragon's feathers as they bend their head to me. Their jaw brushes the floor of the cave so I can touch the sensitive feathers at the crown with my numb hand. Dragons can sense a poet on instinct, and this one, having survived on physical sustenance its entire life, sniffs me as if ready to inhale my past.

I start with the most basic and beautiful thing I remember. "My second mother's name is Brinna."

ON LORE

LOCAL NEWS WAS ABUZZ with stories of the new restaurant on Second Street that folded wishes for demonic possession into their phyllo dough, rinsed lettuce with cursed water, and prescribed personalized nightmares with their seasonal menu.

Lore wanted to try the dream-inducing food during the opening week, but we were too common to afford it. She stalked the restaurant one evening, hoping to peek through garbage they threw out, but there was none. She accosted patrons as they left the restaurant at midnight, posing as press and asking them for their opinions of their dining experience. Patrons had nothing to say to the actual press and certainly nothing to say to Lore. They stared through her and moved in a daze, their hands pressed to their heads the way people put their hands on their bellies after eating too much, as if holding something in.

3AM Eatery caused a fuss with the renovation of its downtown property. *Much too modern,* supporters of historic local architecture mourned. *Uninviting — foreboding, even,* one mother was quoted saying of its façade of one-way windows, dark and mirrored from the outside. *Hard to believe it's going to be a restaurant.*

Owner and head chef Michelle Reed liked to talk in interviews about her education at the finest culinary schools, training abroad, and family recipes. In all her photographs, her grin exposed lines of neatly-filed teeth. Her hair was an unflatteringly vibrant red. People remembered her voice differently:

some said it sounded like gravel; others said they could barely hear her, that she was always whispering. Lore studied reports for who said what about Reed's voice and concluded that they were all right, because how one heard Chef Reed's voice revealed something about the self.

I loved Lore. She dreamed of being a painter but was afraid of being bad at it and so rarely practiced. For two months, she longed to be a model, but agencies told her she was too short and her chin could be sharper. Instead, she opened an online store that sold doilies and puppy mittens and cup holders she crocheted herself. She made a couple sales every week, but there were already people doing it better who had been doing it for longer.

I understood when she became obsessed with 3AM Eatery. Six weeks later, when the excitement over the new restaurant had died down and no one had anything either scathing or remarkable to say about it, Lore managed to reserve a table for us. I knew she hadn't suddenly made a bunch of money with her crochet business and asked if she could afford something like this.

I offered to help them close, she messaged.

You mean you work there? You found a job? Happy for you! I responded. I glanced up from texting under my desk to see nearly half the students texting under their own. At least they were quiet.

Tonight at 11

Oh, that's soon. Haven't thought of an outfit.

Was the last dream you had a good one or a bad one

I don't want to pick up a nightmare there. Just try the food.

Tell me about your dream though

I glanced at the students again. *It was one of those repetitive but terrifying ones. The kind you want to cry about after waking up but laugh about how illogical it is with your friends after.*

But what happened

The principal walked by. I slid the phone into the desk drawer.

I don't remember going into the restaurant or being seated. Menus waited atop the slate tablecloth in front of us, *3AM* boldly burned into the center of their black leather covers. I wasn't sure what kind of food 3AM served. The articles that had come out in the first weeks all said something different. Sometimes the atmosphere was *quaint*, sometimes it was *edgy*. Some people praised the farmhouse décor. Others said they were struck by the use of hard metal edges and glass.

Lore and I stared at the covers of our menus. The patrons around us did the same, none of them moving. 3AM's intimate dinner lighting seemed more in service of creating shadows than a mood so, when I did look up from the menu, I had trouble seeing Lore. I wanted to talk to her, to ask her questions about the new job, to laugh about how we were having our first fancy dinner date two years into our relationship. I wanted to propose moving in together, how she could put her half-dead plants next to my mostly surviving ones on the water-damaged windowsill. I could say how I wanted to help her more. Yes, I'd start that way.

Chef Reed emerged from the darkness at our tableside. She asked us in a whisper-hoarse voice — like something she'd lost screaming herself awake — what we'd like to have. Lore lifted her head and asked for an expansive nightmare, something striking like inspiration.

The kind so vivid you can't shake it off in the daylight, she said, the spark in her eyes the brightest thing in the darkness.

No, Lore, I thought I'd said, but my mouth didn't move, and there was no sound.

Chef Reed smiled. Her teeth were not pointed at all like they were in the pictures. She asked what I would like.

I said I didn't want anything. I suddenly wasn't hungry.

The food here is weightless, she told me, so everyone can indulge.

No, I said.

Chef Reed asked about dessert.

Lore laughed. *Have something. It's on me.*

Yes, on Lore, Chef Reed confirmed.

The tablecloth was red.

We use red as the palette cleanser to prepare the mind for the dream, said Lore, looking just past me into the dimness beyond.

I didn't need to use the restroom, but I told them I did. My chair screeched across the polished concrete floor when I pushed it back, and the noise echoed with nothing soft to absorb it. I fumbled through the darkness, hands out in front of me.

In the women's restroom, two low sofas faced each other. Between them, a marble statue of a malnourished Aphrodite stood upright in a clawfoot tub. There were no stalls or sinks and no door other than the one that led back to the dining room. Except for the spotlight over the statue, the room was dark. I pressed myself against the wall and breathed. I wouldn't ruin this experience for Lore.

Chef Reed was gone when I returned.

I got something small for us to share if you're not that hungry.

Oh good, I said. My hands shook beneath the table.

Chef Reed said I could eat here from now on. I could save so much on groceries.

At the cost of what? I wanted to ask but, again, no sound. The food — Lore's food — suddenly filled the space between us. The white square of her plate overflowed with wool.

The tablecloth was black. *After the palette cleanser, we use black so that you can fall, uninhibited, into the dream*, Lore intoned.

A saucer to the side held a single dark chocolate truffle. Chef Reed appeared with it — not that she'd delivered the food, only appeared simultaneously — and pointed at the dessert with a long finger. She considered it, then said, in my mother's voice, that I seemed like a strawberry kind of girl. The truffle faded to white chocolate with pink swirls. When she looked at me, I tasted overripe fruit, the kind that dimples at the touch and draws flies.

I reached for Lore, but my hand landed in the wool.

I'll share with you, Lore said, her mouth fuzzy.

IN OUR SEASON

W E STEP OFF THE plane together, but while she is coming home, I have never been farther away from mine. No one in the airport—or in the town where we settle into our hotel—looks like us. She squeezes my hand in hers, has nothing but reassuring smiles. Her mother's side of the family is here. I have never met them, but I have seen the family reunion photographs.

Here, in summer, the sun barely sets. She warned me about this before suggesting our trip. I am a brittle insomniac. I haven't dreamed in months. She massages lavender oil into my skin before bed, and now whenever I think of the plant I am transported back to our bed where I lie awake with my restless thoughts. Better though, to face sleeplessness in the land of midnight sun than to endure its near-lightless winters. Rós would never risk a winter trip to Iceland, not with me.

The hotel is nice—a short walk from the sea. I know the sea. I have lived near beaches. But this is not Florida. The sand here is volcanic black and tangled with slimy red plants; mountains rise forever at our backs. After a sleepless jetlagged night, Rós asks me what I think of this coastal town with its brine perfume and cold fishermen, its colorful rooftops dotted among the sharp landscape. I think she is asking what I think of her. I answer in my limited Icelandic vocabulary, and she smiles.

Over a breakfast of skyr and oatmeal, Rós asks me how I would like to begin our vacation. Hot springs? Hiking? She confesses that she's been curious about the now-abandoned US military base, a neighbor to her hometown of Keflavík. Her mother had worked in the school cafeteria on the base, serving food to rowdy American children on the weekdays. As a child, Rós thought this was very impressive and asked her mother all about what life was like on the other side of the gate. Unremarkable, her mother had seemed to think, because most of what she said pertained to her sore feet.

In the past few years—while Rós was away at college, while we built our life together in the US—much of the Keflavík base was converted for civilian use. After all, most of it was family housing and the school. However, one of the condos, the real reason Rós wants to see the base, has remained abandoned. People were scheduled to move in, but all plans were dropped, she says.

I push my spoon into the skyr and sit back. My body is heavy with the sleep it hasn't had. Rós, though, seems unburdened, as if this eternal light feeds her. Her brown skin glows with it.

"So what's with the condos?" I ask. "Mold? Structural issues?"

She leans forward. "Wrong weather."

It is as any other neighborhood. Children play in the grassy fields between the condos. Families leave and return in their cars. Despite the evidence of life, it is quiet. The sun is pale with its light, as if it has reserved its warmer hues for southern latitudes. I feel lulled. I feel unreal. The sky is open.

If here I stare at my feet too much, for once, it's not anxiety. The volcanic rock peeks through patches of grass, a determined reminder of what made this land. Black rock worn to black gravel and, at the coasts, to black sand. I toe a patch of it when we stop walking, grinding my boot into this new earth.

The road winds among red and blue and green rooftops, the sides of each three-story condo the same strange yellow. I follow Rós. She consults no map, just walks determinedly ahead. She will know it when she sees it, she'd said.

Wind pushes, pulls, insistent. It is loud enough in our ears to be a living thing. Rós lets it tug her cardigan while I zip my jacket and pocket my hands. Eventually, she stops in front of one of the condos, and it turns out that I also know *this* is the one. This shadow is different from other summer shadows. This chill feels old, leftover from another time. I look around us. It is noon, and the sun is high. None of the other buildings cast a long shadow, none of them defy physics and light.

Two children have paused their play to watch us. At home, I'd think their staring was a result of seeing two Black girls holding hands, any of the usual things. But here, I know it's because of the building—and Rós' proximity to it.

They shout something quick in unison, something I can't parse with my limited vocabulary.

Rós frowns and looks up into the dark windows. "I will tell you if we find any elves," she responds in English.

The children shake their heads just as Rós steps into the shadow—and falls. I hurry to her side only to feel the ground slip from under me. Suddenly, I am breathless and staring up into a dark and angry sky. Snow whips down on the cutting wind, searing the exposed skin of my cheeks.

"Black ice," Rós yells above the howling wind. She has braced herself against the building and holds one hand down to me. I take it instinctively, still disoriented from landing on my back and having my breath knocked out of me.

I look for the children and find them gone. The cars parked at the condos have vanished. I turn back to Rós and find her vanished from the place she stood. I call for her, I turn around and around, heart kicking into a panicked rhythm. I catalogue the snowdrifts, the storm. Rós' advice comes back to me in her own voice. *Small steps on the ice. Keep your center of gravity level with your feet.*

I cross the sidewalk back into the parking lot, but the storm doesn't abate. Where we'd once stood in summer sunshine, there is suddenly none. I walk to the next condo, the next, but there is no end to the storm. Behind me, I have carved a trail through the snow drifts, and snow dusts my jeans up to my thighs. I am already shivering in my inadequate clothes. The gate we entered through at the base perimeter has become lost in the white out.

There is nothing to do but retreat inside. I know what Rós would say about the severity of Icelandic snowstorms, her quoted statistics about exposure and frostbite. She's told me the stories about how seriously people take the storms, about what can happen if you don't. In the path behind me, the whirlwind of snow parts around a figure in a red cardigan, a beacon in the night. I think—I *think*—I see an arm reaching towards me, a mouth opened wide. I move towards her; the wind doubles down. I put up a hand to shield my face, and when I can look again, she is gone.

Every condo door is locked. I pick my way back through the snow and ice to where we started, leaning into the wind and fighting for each step. With every other glance, the red of Rós' cardigan flutters wild ahead of me, like a bird caught in a trap. I cling to the visual, the only guide in the white-out, as I squint against the assault of snow and icy wind. I turn my head away, and the wind stings my cheek so numb it aches. Streetlamps quaver, their light sickly halos of yellow in the deep dark. Ahead, the doors to the strange condo are open, a beacon in the storm. Within them, light shines. I only hope that Rós has gone this way, that we will reunite at this shelter. I pull the stiff door closed. A sharp metal screech pierces the air, and then the howl of the wind is no longer a deafening thing, a fierce creature muzzled to a low growl. A pile of snow has started to form in the foyer, but being out of the wind's reach is a relief.

I lean against a wall, and only then do I realize how much I'm shaking.

"I'm sorry," says Rós, breathless. She sounds as if she is speaking from a great distance through a distorting fog.

I look up, around, but she isn't here, not quite. She ghosts around the edges of my vision, a smear of motion and red.

I am numb in more ways than one. I realize I should breathe. Try to locate my edges. Rós is here, even if in some faded state. I wish we could hold each other. I do not cry although I wish I could. I am used to one kind of numbness, and that's the one I lean into. It is familiar and therefore a comfort.

Construction supplies and building materials litter the space in front of the stairway. These are heavy things, not the sort of stuff that could be moved without intention. They are scattered as if they were not knocked over but hastily dropped. I do not want to think of what would make someone drop something so heavy, of what would make someone abandon such expensive tools.

The storm outside continues to rage.

Neither of us asks the obvious question. It feels like it might trap us as much as the storm, as much as whatever strangeness pulled us out of our season and into this one.

At least there is light. It feels too dim for the stairway, casting broken geometric shadows through the rails. This place smells like road salt and ice. To the right, there's a room of what looks like post boxes, all neatly shut. Through the window into the room, I see a bulletin board with faded flyers. I can't read them from here.

The door to the post room swings open easily. Here also the light feels too yellow, too inadequate to beat back the oppressive dark. All the flyers are the same, all in plain black and white. In the corner, there's a too-dark image of someone staring out a window. It's one of those pictures that obviously used to be in color but was printed badly to save money on color ink. In large letters, the flyer asks FEELING DOWN? There's a warning about the winter, the long dark and what it can do to people. At the bottom, there are tear-off numbers for a hotline, the bottoms of the flyers jagged with them. I tear one off, another. I recognize the need that has overtaken me—the need for someone to see and affirm the pain, the loneliness—but this feeling is not mine. I stuff them into my pockets as if that will ease the ache in my chest. I snatch a flyer down and crumple it into my jacket pocket. With every move, there's the rasping susurrations of paper. It grows louder, filling the room like the deafening howl of the wind.

Her hand is light on my arm, the touch a question. The papery rustle dies. I step away from the board and breathe out all the tension it'd heaped on me, like expelling a wound. Rós' face is close but blurred. I try to place one of the slips of paper into her faded hand. It passes through and flutters to the floor. I see tension around her eyes; then she's gone. When I look back to the board, all the paper I'd torn down is replaced, but the copy has changed. Only the hotline number remains.

I check my phone and am surprised to find service bars. I try the number for Rós' Icelandic grandmother, who we'd planned to stay with later in our trip. After several faint rings, someone picks up. It is not Rós' grandmother. They give their name and tell me that I've reached a mental health crisis line. I look at the screen and find the number I've dialed is the same as the one on the flyers. I apologize and hang up, try again. I reach the same operator. They do not seem annoyed to hear from me again—either they have forgotten or are just being professional. I apologize again and wander back into the foyer, phone in hand. FEELING DOWN? The flyers have changed again when I glance back. I cannot access the internet. None of my apps will load. All other numbers I try ring and ring without voicemail. FEELING DOWN?

I dial the number on the flyer. It doesn't ring. Immediately, I hear the voice of the operator, the same one, thanking me for calling them. They sound so sincere, so kind, that it hurts. I want to believe that they can help.

"I think—I think I'm. Trapped. Somehow. I'm on the old base..." I begin. The operator expresses confusion. "No, this isn't a mental health emergency, but it is an emergency. I can't seem to reach anyone else. Can you connect me to . . ." The line goes dead when she transfers me. I realize it's not cold enough to see my breath on the air. There must be heat coming from somewhere—but it's still cold.

I step over the strewn tools and construction materials. Up the stairs, something rattles in the wind. A window must be open somewhere. Its whistle is sharp as if squeezed through a small space.

FEELING DOWN?

I recognize the feeling that lives here, though I didn't expect to find it in summer. It lives at the end and beginning of every year, like a bookend to each segment of my life.

I call the hotline number again. "I feel—trapped," I say after the operator thanks me for calling.

"It can feel like that, can't it?" they say. They encourage me to say more. I dig through my memory of previous winters and think of the way my mood predictably darkens with the season. This is what I give. The operator soothes. They name resources and give advice. They say, "The way out is forward."

"What?" I say, even though I heard them fine. I start towards the stairs.

"They way out is forward," they repeat.

"Thank you."

The rail is icy when I lay my hand on it, and I pocket my hands again. I take the stairs up.

At each landing, the hall splits off to the left and right. Two apartments comprise each side. The walls are heavy concrete blocks painted white.

These buildings have the character of something built to withstand and endure, and that is what they offer. There is no softness or art. Nothing to distract one from the way that winter closes in and creeps into the mind.

The doors to the right are bolted shut. To the left, the sustained howl of the wind becomes a sharp whistle. I try the first door and find it locked. The door at the end of the hall, however, rattles in its frame. Cold pushes from under it and settles around my ankles. I find the door unlocked, brace my shoulder against it, and push against the wind. As soon as I'm inside, the wind catches the door and slams it shut behind me, a sharp crack splitting time into before and after.

The hall is dark. To the left, there's the void of a doorway, and at the end, the expanse of a larger room. I venture towards it, peeking into the smaller doorway as I pass. Within, the white outline of a refrigerator is broken up by shadow and the sickly yellow light thrown by the streetlamp, the familiar shapes of its edges smudged soft by the shadow and turned sharp by the light. The large space at the end of the hall turns out to be a living room, although sparsely furnished with what looks to be stiff waiting room chairs. Icy air whips in through the open windows, but I am drawn to circle the chairs, feeling towards the heavy impression inhabiting one of them. I have the urge to reach out and massage nonexistent shoulders, to lean over the person-shaped emptiness and whisper in a shadow ear. The air around me shrieks with wind. I grip the arm of a chair, squeeze the upholstery, and settle myself into the heavy impression on its seat. Or: it settles into me.

I am a list of undone things, the ache of too much restless rest, an anxious craving for foods I don't want. I breathe it in and try not to drown in it. I bring a memory of the eternal sun and the embrace of a loved one. I bring the last undisturbed sleep I had and a memory of sunrise.

The windows behind me snap shut. I open my eyes, not realizing I'd closed them. A boxy television against the far wall flickers on, shining gray light through the room. An afterimage of Rós briefly smears the space beside me.

On the screen, a woman stares out the window from within a dark room. The voiceover asks about sudden changes in mood or behavior in oneself or loved ones. There's a list of symptoms. The PSA ends by flashing a number across the screen, the same one that filled my pockets. The announcement begins to loop before cutting out into static.

The rest of the apartment is filled with similar placeholder furniture—unremarkable, uncomfortable, and sparse. Furniture that has been used by many and loved by none.

On the windowsill of a child's bedroom, I find a smooth, palm-sized lava rock is on the windowsill. I pick it up, turn it over once, twice. I hold it up to the lamplight from the window, and Rós' ghostly hand materializes to point out a smear of paint on one side. A child has tried to paint a flower. Someone has found joy in this landscape. I hold to it, turn it over in my hand like a worry stone.

I climb the stairs to each floor and find the doors where the wind rushes in, the places where emotional impressions have settled deep into a space—the sunken center of a mattress, in front of a bathroom mirror, at a window overlooking a frozen playground. I inhabit each and give to them and try not to let my own feelings overtake me. I squeeze the stone in my hand. I remember Rós—to remember love and to give love. I have to believe that I'll find her again.

The way out is through.

On the third and final floor, the wind is loudest. The lights in the hall have gone out. From the landing, the windows into the condo's common room are black mirrors. I don't think of myself as a superstitious person, but I am reluctant to look into them. I am struck with the fear that I might see the personifications of the impressions I have encountered—unfamiliar ghostly faces smudged by time. I try to walk past, but my attention is drawn.

No, the impressions are soothed. They are no longer here. When I look, there is only the smudged reflection of my own face. I step towards it as if that might resolve the reflection into something familiar. Instead, Rós appears beside me, clear for the first time since we fell into winter. I don't turn, knowing that if I do, she will be gone. It seems that she sees me as well, and we make eye contact in the glass. She points down one of the halls and disappears.

There's no need to check all the doors on this floor. The wind and the remaining presence are enough of a signal. In this last apartment, the outside lamplight doesn't shine though the windows. I find the open window in the bedroom.

I crawl into the space, and it immediately pulls me under, starving for comfort and companionship. They have gone so long unseen and unheard that they do not know what to ask. They have lost how to name the thing consuming them.

I roll over (when did I lay down?) and it is an effort with a body so weighted. Rós is at the bedside with tea. She tries to smile at me and sets it on the coaster. She gives me a warm blanket fresh from the dryer and takes the old one away. The emptiness presses tears into my eyes. I could cry for them.

I wake up (when did I fall asleep?) and Rós is making soft clattering noises in the kitchen. I picture her taking down plates from the cupboard. The house smells faintly sweet. She appears in the doorway with a plate of breakfast.

I pull on an oversized shirt. The light in the room is different. Late evening sunset limns the edges of the curtains. I realize I am back in our bedroom at home. My skin smells of lavender. Rós has coaxed the tension out of my shoulders. I turn to thank her and find her gone. I begin to doubt she was ever here. But there is her impression in the sheets. I go looking for her, but the apartment is wrong. Our rooms are not here, not laid out like this. I trail my hand along the wall of the hall, and it turns cool and stony under my fingertips. I call out for Rós. The furniture in the living room is not the eclectic antiques Rós picked out. They are plain and worn. Dull navy in the evening light. All wrong colors. I throw open the curtains, and it is abruptly night. Sickly yellow light falls across the floor.

I am in bed (when did I crawl back into bed?), and I can't move. I curl my fingers against the bare mattress and find the stone still in my grasp. There are no more fresh blankets or steaming tea. I am alone in an empty room, and I have lost time. The storm still surges.

"You have to let me go," I say to the emptiness. "I have shown the others peace, and they let me go."

It presses down, insistent. My chest feels full of water. I understand.

By the end of winter, crying feels impossible. Sometimes it's not sadness but numbness that overwhelms.

I let the water surge, tighten my throat, press behind my eyes. These are another person's tears, but I welcome them as if they are my own. The pressure abates, and I am able to move just as full-body sobbing has my body curling in on itself. I am lost in it, and through the loss I find my own fresh fear—that there is no end to this, that I will exist as this grayer, weaker version of myself forever. That I will not escape winter and that no one would weather it with me.

"Isa?"

She is a specter, but she is here. Rós looks as shocked to see me as I am to see her. She reaches out to me, but our realities are desynchronized, and our hands pass through each other.

"Rós," I say, just as she opens her mouth and is gone.

I am alone again, fully alone. The pressure has been soothed and is departed. My face is puffy, and the chill raises new goosebumps on my skin, but I am lighter. I can take a full breath.

The building is settled. I emerge from the final apartment to find the world on the other side of the threshold quieter, but not only for the lack of wind-rattled doors. Now, it is truly quiet, the passing of a storm.

I return to the common room, its windows still wide and dark but silvery with moonlight. It contains the same stiff office furniture as the rest of the building, but there's a shimmer of color that draws me in. I step around the dark masses of furniture and to the window.

Ribbons of teal and emerald light thread through the dissipating storm clouds. The beast in the wind has retreated. The sky is opening. Perhaps, perhaps this is the other side. On the ground below, I spot a flutter of red.

I tear down the steps. Some are slick with melted snow, but I grip the rail and keep running, each step a frantic squeak. Through the glass-paneled doors, I see Rós. She stands with her back to me, cardigan drawn tight around her as she looks up at the colored sky. I pull the door open, and the screech of its hinges draws her attention to me. I have forgotten about the ice, and so has she. We are falling into each other's arms—and into sunlight.

We land hard on the pavement, but we will check for bruises later. For now, we are speaking over each other, hands finding one another again and again. Gripping a shoulder, cupping a face, threading fingers through hair. The sun shines down. We are back in our season.

Rós is smiling, smoothing a hand down my side when she pauses and pats at my pocket. She withdraws the painted lava rock, and her expression falls at the sight of it. Her gaze flicks back to me.

"It was real," I say.

She looks back to the building. Its shadow has retreated to something natural. "I don't want to think that it was," she says.

We stand. I think she might throw the rock, but for now, it remains clenched tight in her hand. I look back at the condo. Rós doesn't. She's too focused on me.

"Will you be okay? Should we go home? Should I—" She gestures vaguely, drops her hands to her sides.

The sun hasn't moved in the sky. The children—still staring—stand where they last did, but I feel like I have moved through so much time. I shiver the early winter away.

THE FUTURE IN SALT WATER

T HE GOD TURNED A soothing shade of black upon touching me for the first time and wrapped its eight suckered arms securely around my forearm. Cool temple air combined with its damp skin, and I shivered. I was not a strong child, but Cheypa, my parent, smiled down on me proudly for bearing the god's weight so well. The bulbous mantle of its body flattened as it sunk the needle of its beak into the soft flesh of my inner elbow. I winced.

Luo—the god spoke my new name into my mind, simultaneously pulling out the memory of my old name like blood from a vein. *I want to see the ocean*, it said, undulating and boneless. My heart sank at this first request. On the way to the temple, my parent had told me that their god's first request had been to acquire water from one of the inland freshwater lakes and pray over it until it turned to salt water. I wanted such a simple first task. My god's request would mean not only abandoning my ill parent but also walking for days in the dangerous heat, only to confirm the still-toxic state of the ocean water.

Two temple acolytes who'd been standing at the ready noticed my wince and hurried over to begin painting sacred scripts down my godless arm. The black ink was chilled, as Ocean specified, and the brush tickled my skin. I suppressed another shiver, but my skin prickled. "What name did your god give you?" the acolytes asked in whispered unison. They were intent on their job and spared me no glance.

"Luo," I answered.

All that remained was to paint my new name across my palm. The acolytes sat back and stared into the clay bowl of ink, divining the unique symbol that would represent my new name. As we waited for the symbol to manifest, sections of ink trailed down my arm, one cold word drifting into another. The two acolytes moved in a trance, hands and brushes a blur as they painted my name. The ink in place, they said, "An honour to meet you, Luo," and backed away with their clay bowl and brushes.

I looked at my palm in the dim temple light. Three circles: two concentric, the third intersecting both. Some ink had already passed through my skin and done its work to numb the site where the god's beak had pierced me. The god was silent now, but its arms undulated in reassurance. My parent smiled and patted the too-tight rows of braids they'd done the night before in preparation for the ceremony. We would not talk until we'd left the temple. Custom dictated that the newly named listen and talk only to their god while on sacred ground.

I glanced around the temple's main hall before we turned to leave, hoping to catch sight of the reclusive Temple Mother. I would not see her that day either. Few people had ever seen her. If she did not make an appearance for the naming rituals, there weren't many other important events she might appear for. Children liked to spread rumours that they'd seen her in the shadows, watching their naming, but then who didn't want to imagine the Temple Mother gracing them with her attention?

This time, as we passed through the hall of water that led to the outer doors, I looked up through the glass to watch the unpaired gods spiralling through the blue. My god had settled on skin black as the ceremonial ink itself, but the ones that swam around us flashed colours I'd only glimpsed on the garments of rich travellers visiting the market. Before we passed through the temple doors, my parent pulled their goggles down over their eyes and tapped my shoulder to remind me to do the same. My god shifted so I could bend my arm, and then we were out and into the blinding sun.

Following the quiet cool of the temple, I was unprepared for the assault of noise and heat and light. My parent could not afford a vehicle or riding animal, and so we would sweat on the walk home while rich travellers in sand skiffs and more modest traders with animal-drawn carriages sped past us on the dusty street. Sometimes I could successfully beg a trader to let us ride with them toward central New Limsa. Often ill, my parent didn't fare well in the strength-sapping heat. We waved at a couple of passing carts, but the most we got was the blank stare of their mirrored goggles, reflecting our sweaty, dusty figures back at us. Cheypa kept saying we would go to a glass weaver to repair my own cracked goggles, but that promise had first been made many moons ago, and the left glass was still cracked across its horizon.

The god withdrew its beak, slithered up my arm and onto my head to clap the end of an arm across the broken lens. When it slid back down to my shoulder, the crack was gone and my goggles dripped water. Thanks to the ink, I did not feel pain when it anchored its beak into the flesh between my shoulder and collarbone, re-establishing our connection. *Thank you*, I said, but my gratitude felt inadequate. The god snaked its arms around my neck. An embrace. Its damp skin felt like a cool rag around my shoulders, a balm in the heat.

A woman with an intricately wrapped scarf on her head stared at me from the back of a merchant caravan. From her closely tailored clothes, I guessed she was from one of the cooler, central lakeside cities. Their caravans rarely travelled this far south toward the poisoned, heated ocean, and they did not understand the concerns of previously seaside cities that were forced inland, away from their water. The lakesiders did not believe in the gods; rather, they did not believe our octopoda possessed fractions of Ocean's consciousness. Though they liked to come to New Limsa to trade fine goods with our unrivaled glass weavers, they didn't understand the Oceanic teachings behind the beautiful glass.

My parent stepped in front of me to shield me from the prying eyes of the lakesider who had called more of her people over to come look at the strange child with an ocean creature around their neck. Near home, Cheypa's sandals scraped the street; they sagged against my godless shoulder. I scanned us into the small box of our ground-level apartment and the sand, as always, swept in with us. The door beeped, hissed shut. We crunched across the floor. I put my god in a shallow bowl we'd left out on the altar. The best water we had, our drinking water, was brown and not at all like the crystalline sparkle of the hall of water in the temple, but this was what we had to offer my god. I poured slowly so as not to splash any. The god, relieved to be in water again, squished its arms in close so they were all submerged. Cheypa gave me a smile as they passed and went to lay down on their cot in the corner of the room. They were always so tired. Even their time with their god as a child had not cured them of what the temple acolytes called their "weak heart fire."

We had one high narrow window in our apartment, and so despite the blinding desert light, it was always dim inside. The electric lights were expensive and thus saved for detailed work. New Limsa might have been known for its glass weavers, but that did not mean that most of our own people could afford much glass. Cheypa was not bothered by this, had said the dark indoors reminded them of their years of service in the windowless temple.

To the ocean. Soon, said the god.

I glanced at my parent, breathing shallow on their cot. *Who will care for them when they're tired? Cook when they can't? Complete the ornaments for market?*

The ocean is always first. The god's black skin shifted toward grey.

Could you heal Cheypa's heart like you healed my goggles? Then I could go and not worry.

Your devotion is admirable, but Cheypa will not be forgotten.

We have no money to hire a skiff or even rent a riding animal. And no one would permit someone to take their animal near the ocean.

A pause. *Luo.* The god spoke my new name alone, and I averted my eyes. *The ocean is always first.*

I kneeled at the small altar so that I didn't have to speak. Ours was not as elaborate as those at the temple—platforms of glass in pools of water. One could wade in and almost imagine stepping into the wash of the clean ocean. In our home, we had a simple sandstone block with a glass cup of blessed saltwater on top. Each week, we tucked a new prayer slip into the small corked vial at the bottom of the saltwater. At the end of the moon, we returned the saltwater to the hall of water and drew a new cup.

I reached into the cup for the vial. Cheypa had said I could change the prayer by myself for the first time when we returned with my god. I removed the old slip of paper and took a new one to write, *Strengthen my parent's heart fire.* This was not a new prayer. I'd often asked Cheypa to pray for their own health. They'd been reluctant to do so but always wanted to make sure they acknowledged my input on household prayers.

This was not a new prayer, but now there was a god on our altar.

I took Cheypa water and started grinding spices for dinner. Put beans to simmer low over the gas fire. In minutes, the room was filled with aromatic warmth.

Cheypa dozed, their face dappled with sweat, carefully set curls frizzing back out into kinks. I was laying a cool damp cloth against their forehead when my god said, *They would not be alone. The temple would make sure of that.*

I did not look at the altar. I tasted the beans. Needlessly crushed more cardamom pods. The beans were already well-spiced.

I won't abandon Cheypa like Doni did, I said.

Doni had been the strong one in our family. Doni had abandoned us for the promise of a lakeside city shortly after receiving the ink of passage. We received less contact from her over the years. The last communication had been moons ago, about a joining ceremony with a lakesider. It wasn't an invite, only a statement. Not that Cheypa could have made the journey anyway.

I ate alone, sour now that I'd reminded myself of Doni. Cheypa still slept, and I did not want to wake them. I set aside their portion of dinner for later.

The god spoke again when I was settling into my cot. *Decades have passed since I've seen the ocean.* Their longing begged for an answer. My chest tightened. A splash in the dark from the direction of the altar.

I covered my head with blankets. Turned over.

Lungs, chest full of damp weight. My stomach churned. I stumbled out of my cot and fell to the concrete floor. Small morning light in the window. Cheypa's blankets rustled as they turned over in sleep. I crawled to the altar. Tried to take a breath.

The octopoda.

I stared.

The small light must be lying.

I fumbled for the light plate on the wall. It beeped at the touch of my hand. White-blue light hummed down.

The octopoda.

Water gone from the bowl. The godform. Grey, desiccated.

I pointed a shaking finger toward the mantle. Touch caved in papery skin. Bitter snap. Shivering breath in silence. My breath my lungs.

And the ink on my skin—vanished. As if there'd been no ritual at all. No naming. The god had taken the memory of my old name, and the new one was gone too. I thought I could remember the way the sound moved, but the specifics were fading.

I was nameless.

I took the bowl from the altar. It was too light. Such a heavy light thing. A noise in my throat.

Cheypa turned over.

I crushed the bowl to my chest and ran, beeped the door open. As it hissed closed, I thought I heard Cheypa utter a sound that could have been my name.

Through the streets, dodging cartwheels and whirring skiffs. Sand stuck in the damp on my cheeks. Someone cried out, I stumbled, fell atop the god. The bowl rolled into the street. A hoof came down. Another. The clay bowl was crushed to dust.

"Let me help you." Brown hand in front of my face. A woman with an inked forehead, a new adult, stared down at me.

I scrambled up and tried to scoop the god into my arms. Its fragile skin crushed into my tunic like dust. Intact, though, was an arm. One. I gingerly picked it up.

The woman was staring. "Is that—?"

I ran.

Breathless, I slammed through the temple's heavy double doors. The clap echoed down the hall of water. Octopoda stopped their placid spiralling and hung in the water in shock. Temple acolytes were immediately upon me, hushing me: "This is the Temple Mother's meditation hour," and "Careful of the glass!" Delayed, I noticed the pain in my side from shouldering open the door.

My mouth was dry with dust and sand. So much of my octopoda had been crushed and whisked away by the wind when I fell. The thin membrane of some of the suckers on its remaining arm had started to crumble. "My god!" I said, holding it up for the others to see.

The temple acolytes stared at my skin, my hair, my clothes, all a dusty mess, uncomprehending.

"My god has— I think my god is—"

A splash sounded behind us, and we turned as one toward the central pool at the end of the hall. One acolyte thought to usher me forward, but now I did not want to move. Their grip was tight on my shoulder at one of the places where the god had pierced me yesterday, but now the site hurt like a wound.

A dark hand gripped the stone edge of the pool, then another. A black-clad figure hauled themselves from the depths. The Temple Mother. Long braids swung heavy with water. Lengths of fabric hung stiff and trailed behind her. Skin, hair, clothes dripping water, leaving a trail of darkened stone in her wake.

She appraised me with eyes the colour of the lost clean ocean. I had never seen someone like us with eyes like hers. Some of the rare pale merchants had blue eyes, but none as blue as hers. None as blue as oceans. So struck by her, I almost forgot the desiccated arm in my grip.

Until she said, "I've never known a child to kill a god."

The Temple Mother took me to a small inner room and asked me to recount all that had happened. She'd taken the arm from me and cradled it like a child.

I could not tell if she was angry or not. Two candles on the table, lone sources of light, cast shadows across her dark face. She sat like a statue and did not blink. She'd not bothered to change her soaked robes, did not even seem to notice that they were wet.

The temple air still felt too cold. I struggled to hold her gaze.

"You refused your god its request?"

"I didn't— I didn't refuse, I just . . ."

"You told them you would not go to the ocean."

I looked down to my lap. "I told them I wouldn't leave my parent alone."

"That is refusal. You are not careful with your words."

I bit the inside of my cheek. Clenched my hands in my lap. "I'm sorry."

"I've never seen this. I've never known someone to refuse a first request. I've also never known a god to ask something so dangerous of a child. Ocean must have thought highly of you, but the force of your denial ruined this godform. I will not entrust you with another."

The candle flames flickered, smoked, steadied.

Without the god years, I would never get the ink of passage. I would never be considered an adult. No one would take me as an apprentice to learn their trade, and I would never be able to support Cheypa as I had planned. One decree from the Temple Mother and my future fell to dust.

"I will not entrust you with another," she repeated, "but you must restore this one. Losing godforms weakens an already frail Ocean."

"How do I heal them?" I asked. Eager, mouth dry.

"When Ocean was young, they were strengthened by sacrifice that melded the human and the divine. They are strengthened by expressions of love and beauty." The Temple Mother returned the dried arm to me. "You have altered the course of your journey so that I cannot predict its path. Now you must interpret these things. Ask Ocean for guidance."

I did not look at the arm. "But how can I ask if my god is . . . gone?"

"Ask *Ocean* for guidance. Not the smaller consciousness of the godform."

"I thought you were the only one who could talk directly to Ocean."

"I think Ocean will be looking to hear from you now."

The Temple Mother guided me to the meditation pool she'd emerged from only an hour before. Her cold hand on my back, she gestured to the pool. "Rest until you have answers."

I nodded, though questions spun my thoughts. She took the arm again. I sat at the edge of the shining pool. Swung my legs over and into the water. Let go and sank. The bubbles of my exhale tickled my face as I kicked to the pool floor. I swam a slow, lazy circle around the perimeter. I didn't need to breathe.

The shadow of the Temple Mother withdrew from the edge of the pool, and I was alone.

When Ocean spoke, they spoke in image. An ornate glass-woven vessel. A heart beating outside its body. The grey arm. Together in the saltwater of the vessel.

Cheypa sat upright on their cot when I returned. Their pouf of hair was flattened on one side. "Where is your god? Why are you soaked?"

"I was at the temple."

"That answers neither of my questions. And you left the light on while you were gone! Do you know what that will cost us?"

"I'm sorry."

"You will explain. Explain everything."

"I lost my god."

Cheypa put their hand to their chest and stood.

"I lost my god and I talked to the Temple Mother and then I talked to Ocean and now I have to make a sacrifice."

Cheypa shook their head and didn't stop.

"I can restore the god I lost."

"Ocean has not asked for a sacrifice in decades! And you are a child. What can you offer?"

The vision Ocean had given was clear. I told Cheypa. I said I didn't think it would hurt. I felt calm about the image of the heart.

"I will talk to the Temple Mother," said Cheypa, moving for the door.

"I want to try."

"You didn't want to go to the ocean, but you will take your heart out? I will surely lose you now." They returned to their cot. "Why does Ocean demand death?"

"It's not death. It's something else." I tried to find the right words for how the images had felt, but my mind fed me images of water arcing, leaping for the sky. I couldn't translate them, so I said again, "I want to try."

Not even legends existed about anyone putting their heart in a glass jar of saltwater. When I went to the glass-weavers' corridor in the market, none understood my request. "I need a jar that will hold my heart," I told them. Some showed me elaborate vases. The most practical among them offered me squat jars meant for storing food for many seasons. The last glass-weaver I found was at the end of the lane, her cart shadowed by a tall building.

Her glass creations spiralled like windstorms and surged up from their bases in waves of colour. They were not containers or jewellery or windowpanes as the others had.

"What are they for?" I asked, reaching out and letting my hand hover near a spike of translucent green.

The woman's arm bangles clinked as she moved. She was younger than my parent but not a child. She wore the face ink of an adult who had only recently returned their god to the temple.

"Joy," she said.

"I mean, what do you use them for?"

She smiled and stepped around her cart so that the array of coloured glasses no longer fractioned and magnified her face. "Are you here for a gift, perhaps?" But then she stopped. "You're the child from the street yesterday!"

I took a step back.

"No, no, don't leave. Are you okay?"

"I need to buy a jar."

"Did you come to the market with a parent?"

"My parent is too sick for the market." I glanced back at her wares. "Will you help me? I need something like a jar. Something that can shut. But also, it should be pretty."

She disappeared behind her wares again, carefully setting aside crates and wrapping and unwrapping the scarves she used to cushion each piece. She came back with a cool sphere and dropped it in my hand. Inside the glass, an orange seashell, forever suspended. I could almost close my hand around it.

I marvelled at the trinket, turning the glass in the light, peeking inside the sloping fissure in the shell as if something might still live there.

"Now for this jar? I don't have anything like that, but I could make it."

"I don't have much money, but I could work for you to pay for the piece. If that would be okay."

She looked me over again. "You seem young. Around the age you would receive your god."

I hesitated. "I did. Two days ago."

"Where is your ink? Where is your octopoda?"

"I made a mistake. Now I need something beautiful to make it up to Ocean."

"To provide for Ocean is payment enough. If you give me three days, I will craft for you a work of art."

"I will not go with you to the temple this time," Cheypa said on the morning of the ritual. They kept their gaze on their beadwork. "I can't see you through this. I can't see you do this."

"I understand."

"I don't know why the Temple Mother is allowing this. It's not tradition." They yanked at the thread and fed another clear bead along the line. "The lakesiders already think we're—" An untied portion slipped and scattered beads across the floor. Cheypa clapped their hands into their lap and huffed. I picked up the fallen beads and poured them into the cup of Cheypa's waiting hands. Their lips trembled. They squeezed their eyes shut.

"I'll be okay. I'll come back. I *promise*."

Cheypa put their beadwork aside. I left with the glass-weaver's jar safely cushioned in my pack.

The entire way to the temple, I kept my hands over my heart.

A sensation like rising, like swimming up, like being buoyed by water, filled my chest. And there was my heart, beating, beating, beating with each step. Here was Ocean. Visions rose like bubbles to the water's surface, a mosaic of past and—future? A city by a clear ocean. I did not know if this was Old Limsa or Limsa to-be.

The Temple Mother stood at the doors when I arrived. I'd never seen her outside. She did not sweat, only glowed in the sun. She did not shield her eyes with goggles, didn't blink, didn't squint. Her robes pooled around her feet in the dust, and her braids, as before, dripped water.

Locals bowed to her. Travellers stared. She acknowledged none of them.

I took her hand when she offered it, and we entered the cool dark of the temple. She told me I had nothing to fear, removed a bundle of cloth from her robes, and unrolled it at the edge of the pool, revealing three knives of different shapes and sizes. I went for the jar in my pack in order to avoid looking at them and held out the swirl of glass to her. She admired how its curves caught the candlelight; the blue of her eyes seemed even brighter when I saw them through the glass.

"The water will accept you now," she said.

I woke in the temple's central pool. My chest was light but not pained, and there was no evidence of incision. Cool water lapped my skin. The Temple Mother loomed statuesque at the edge of the pool. Between her hands, the glass-weaver's jar—and inside that, my still-beating heart. I sensed the black octopoda, restored, on her shoulder before it moved its arms, climbing down to wrap itself around the jar. *Depths*, it whispered to my heart, conveying Ocean's new name for me. I grasped the edge of the pool as I'd seen the Temple Mother do, and the water seemed to push me up, to lend me its strength. I splashed out onto land like a sea creature having just gained legs. The Temple Mother gave me the jar, and I was instantly steadied.

"Keep it close," she said, then reached again into one of the folds of her robe and withdrew a string of beads. I instantly recognized the style, the pattern. I could pick out a piece made by Cheypa in any market display. The pattern was the distinctive alternating black and red given to new adults leaving home for the first time. A blessing. The Temple Mother slipped the necklace over my head with the ceremony of a coronation.

"See them before you leave," she said. "We will care for them at the temple while we await your return." And then she bowed to me, fully kneeling so that we were the same height.

I walked into the desert, clutching the jar against my chest and occasionally glancing down to marvel at how the heart still dutifully beat. Cheypa's beads clicked against the glass with every step. The octopoda, carefully bundled in a sling of scarves, nestled against the glass.

Old Limsa's skeleton broke the horizon.

I pulled along a small cart that held our rowboat. We'd brought no provisions. Would not need them.

Cheypa'd been confused, had tried to give me dried fruits and hard flatbreads for the trip. They'd wondered where I would restock. How I could carry enough drinking water. I'd held their hands, and they'd stopped fretting and said, *You have eyes like the Temple Mother. You're beyond us. No longer a child. Not a human at all, are you?*

I would row across the ocean, and when it was clear, I would come back for Cheypa. I would carry them to the clean water and make them strong.

You're not Ocean, but you're next to the divine. Your presence is heavy and fluid like water.

I am Depths.

Cheypa'd backed away, tried to bow, but I gathered them in a hug.

During my human life, I never knew the sea as anything other than a grey-green mire, but now the possibility of what it could be flashed in my mind like a memory: rippling, ecstatic blue like the lakesider women's scarves in the wind. For that future, I had the strength to row forever.

AT THE MOUTH OF THE SEA

THEY DO NOT CALL themselves mermaids, but that is what we call them. I hope the one I've fallen in love with will stay even though I know she won't. None of them ever do.

They arrive yearly on the way to their pilgrimage sites, and we know they've come by the way the sea beneath our small fishing boats vibrates with song. This is the first year I've been old enough to join the secretive courtship ritual. The village elders allow us girls to do this before we come of age, secure in the knowledge that mersong has never lured a girl away, that, ultimately, young mermaids visit our beach out of curiosity and owe devotion only to the spirit of the sea.

No mermaid has ever visited our shores twice, but that doesn't dim the hope in the older girls' eyes as we stand along the beach, waiting. Until they come of age, many will visit the beach hoping to see their beloved again, only to fall for the charm of another. We are all sick for their affection: the taste of the salt on their lips, their rainbow slicks of hair, the thrill of kissing someone with so many rows of sharp teeth.

Our mothers understand the call to the sea because they have felt it themselves, never stop feeling it. Before we go to meet the mermaids for the first time, our mothers tell us stories of their lost beloveds and caress our hair and give us sad smiles even as they wish us happiness.

The first thing Aaeyeli does is teach me how to sing her name. I am shy about it. I have a poor singing voice. I tell her this. She kisses me and, until the sun sets, her enchantment holds. I find my voice is beautiful like hers, and we speak only in mersong. When the sun rises, Aaeyeli teaches me to swim. Despite being a seaside village, this is not something we teach each other. It is a gift to learn firsthand from someone who has lived in the sea their entire life and will continue to live in it even after our short lives have ended. Aaeyeli says to close my eyes and remember always that the sea spirit wants to embrace our bodies and lift them up, that as long as I remember this, I will not sink.

The next day, I teach her to walk on the shifting sands. Mermaids are immortals and, within certain limits, can shift the forms of their bodies according to their will. Regardless of how long Aaeyeli frowns and studies my legs, however, the ones she forms are too long and jointless. She towers over me. I do not know how to advise on this, so I show her diagrams of human skeletons. I point at the bones, where they connect, how they bend. I bend my own knees to show her. "Ah," she says and makes the middle of her new legs rubbery. I smile and say she'll get the hang of it.

Aaeyeli is delighted by fire and trees and wind. Her eyes are bright and hungry as she watches me eat despite insisting that she doesn't need physical nourishment. We go out on my family's small boat and float along the coast, always in sight of the village. She sits with her fin in the water and rests her head on the side of the boat so that her hair trails through the water, a wave of lavender in the blue. Her skin is brown like ours, but in the noonday sun, it shimmers as if dotted with small gold disks.

Even on this peaceful day, my chest tightens as I look at her. The mermaids only ever stay for a moon, never longer. The easy days make me restless while Aaeyeli is content to float and stroll and drift.

"Do you not want to know me?" I snap one day.

Aaeyeli rolls over from sunning her back, the wet sand plastered to the flat, featureless plane of her chest. Her brow wrinkles. "I do know you. I have watched your body move through water and air. The tempo of your heart and the prints of your feet in the sand tell me you are eager for life. I like this about you."

"But you've never told me anything about yourself, your family. You've never asked me about my family or my mother and the mermaid she loved and how my mother will miss her forever."

"I see." She relaxes back into the sand. "You know I must go. We all do."

"Why?" I am not ready to go back to relaxing and flirting.

At my challenge, Aaeyeli sits up. "If I do not complete the pilgrimage, I will never be an adult among my people. If I stay, you will not live your life and have your own family."

"I don't want a family. I want you. Please, after the pilgrimage, won't you come back?"

She begins to shake her head and I cannot bear it. I kiss her and suddenly we are in the sand and careless when I feel the sting of a cut and taste blood in my mouth. Aaeyeli untangles herself from me, full of apologies. The blood keeps filling my mouth. I see the red on her sharp teeth, smeared across her lips. She wipes it away, stands, and wanders into the cresting waves.

I try to enjoy our remaining days. Aaeyeli's touch becomes lingering; her movements are slow as if time might favor her and do the same. I realize that we fought not because she wants to leave but because she too wants to stay. We do not talk about the blood or the fear blooming wild in my chest. When the day comes, I join the girls of my village on the beach and watch the glitter of mermaid scales as they swim away from us forever.

Our mothers treat us like fragile things when the absence of the mermaids is fresh. I spend so much time in the water that my skin seems always wrinkled and my hair becomes brittle from the salt.

I want to understand the devotion that took her away. I have feverish dreams of taking my family's sailboat and embarking on some destinationless course. I swim until I think I imagine the voice of the sea. All us girls do. Our hope churns the shore of the village, girl limbs chopping up the sea like a storm. I want to understand devotion. I go home and find my mother in the kitchen, back turned to me as she bends over some old family recipe. I embrace her from behind. Into the fabric of her dress, I say, "Will you tell me about when you were seasick?"

She says it's slightly different for everyone and invites me to tell her about my mermaid first. "My mermaid," she says, and that's when I realize how long I've been holding onto my tears, this growing ocean I'd kept secret. My mother's hands smell of fresh-ground spices when she wipes my cheeks dry, and I speak Aaeyeli's name with another human for the first time.

There is a scar on my lip from her, the only evidence that her body touched mine. Sometimes when the tide goes out, I lay on my back in the wet sand and imagine the inside of my mouth is sharp and dangerous like hers.

A Vision of Moonlight

Another moonstruck advisor from last night's lunar viewing party stumbled onto the factory floor in the middle of our shift. All of us factory girls paused, watched, telescope pieces in hand. He staggered past the table of polishers where Adal and I were stationed that day, pointed up to the glass ceiling, and exclaimed in wordless awe. Mouth and eyes wide. Balancing on one tiptoed foot as if he might levitate straight into the void of space to be closer to Sao, Neptune's psychotropic moon.

The moonstruck were a regular sight, but each time I was mesmerized by the stranger's bliss as if by looking closely enough at their eyes, I might also know what it was like to feel good and happy. The factory managers descended. We turned quickly back to polishing our mirrors and lenses, setting glass into sockets. They'd escort the advisor outside and make sure he got a transport back to the chancellor's headquarters. And so another happy customer of the Bliss Viewer Telescope would depart. Another person stunned by a glimpse of Sao.

"I talked to one of the blue-robes," Adal whispered when the outer door slammed shut behind the managers.

I stopped. Glanced at her, then down at the mirror in her hands. Its circle distorted her face so that the pale rainbow sheen of her eyes was all I could see. "You promised you wouldn't—"

The door to the observation deck opened, and another manager started down, staring at Adal the entire way to the factory floor. I turned back to my work, heart pounding for Adal.

The girls who talked to the blue-robed cultists were the ones we never saw again. A week after the first cultist was spotted in district C5, a pattern emerged. The blue-robes approached first. Their targets were factory girls with moonstone eyes, girls like Adal whose eyes reminded us of the seductive curve of lunar satellites we couldn't afford to look at. Some who had witnessed the cultists lure a moonstone-eyed girl into the wilderness said their robes smelled like clean water, that they offered two silver strips of holofilm in one hand and fresh-cut night-blooming flowers in the other. For two days, Adal had smelled like water and flowers. For two days, she'd kept a secret.

That Adal was the last moonstone-eyed girl in C5 was not a secret. No one said so, but everyone was waiting for the moment she'd disappear, charmed by the promises of exotic strangers who drank clean water and cultivated living plants.

The factory managers, though they tried to treat all of us like interchangeable cogs, watched Adal more closely. Like all moonstone-eyed people, she could discern perfection with a glance and was therefore valuable for any tasks requiring precision. For them, her value was the same as a piece of state-of-the-art equipment, another attraction perfect for the daytime factory tours.

Tourists dressed in the vibrant, clean garments of B-district citizens filed after the returning managers. A couple dozen guests today. One of the larger groups that had toured the factory in the past few weeks. Their heeled boots clicked across the factory's concrete floor as they headed for the catwalk. These were people who could obtain better work than us C5 citizens but still didn't have enough credits to attend a viewing party and take home a Bliss Viewer telescope of their own. Watching us assemble them was the closest they'd ever get to the experience.

Two women and a manager broke off from the group and came towards the polishers' table, towards me and Adal. I tensed, wadding the polishing cloth up in my fist. The tourists breathed awe, raising hands glittering with gems to their faces.

"Can we?" one said, extending a greedy hand towards Adal. The manager pulled Adal around the table and in front of the tourists.

They gripped her chin and turned her head as if inspecting a piece of merchandise. Tapped her eyes with their fingernails and exclaimed about how her eyes were "genuine stone, the real artifact!" Marveled at how beautifully the sunlight played across the moonstone. They leaned in too close, hands hovering over her face as if they were entertaining the idea of plucking out her eyes to wear as fashionable statement jewelry. I set aside the glass, not quite polished to standard, for fear of shattering it in my grip.

Alerted by the too-heavy clink of glass against glass, the manager shot me a look. Hands shaking, I pretended to need a fresh cloth and bent to inspect the crates of neatly folded linens beneath the table. The manager ushered the tourists back to the main group.

I'd stopped asking if Adal was okay after these encounters—not because I didn't care but because I knew she wasn't. I handed her a polishing cloth and used it as an opportunity to give her hand a clandestine squeeze. "I'm sorry," I whispered. It was all I could safely give for now.

Transparent panels composed the upper half of the building, and during the tours, the managers liked to brag that they managed one of the only C5-level factories that really cared about the conditions of its workers, allowing us to work the daylight half of our shifts under natural light. But the real reason for the glass was the nighttime viewing parties.

Government enforcers and chancellor advisors waited outside every evening to be invited in by the managers. The enforcers and advisors liked to watch the managers line us up and pat us down for any telescope parts we might have tried to smuggle out in our jumpsuits.

Months ago, a group of girls had managed to assemble half a telescope with stolen parts, and the managers let this go on for a couple weeks in order to make a big show of letting the enforcers stun and drag them away one evening. No one else tried to steal anything after that, but the managers sometimes liked to single out the most nervous among us for questioning. A pre-viewing show for the amusement of the chancellor's men.

I was the one selected that evening.

I was almost to the door. Adal was behind me. A manager scanned my eyes for identification purposes. Hands shaking, I stared ahead at the door. The head manager patted me down and pretended to draw a small lens from my sock. Adal and the girl in front of me saw him palm the glass from where he'd tucked it up in his sleeve, but we all stayed still and silent. The manager turned to the crowd of enforcers and advisors and waved the glass so that it caught the light of the overhead lamps. Two of the enforcers stepped forward, going for the stunners at their hips. I felt my heartbeat in my mouth, in my ears.

"I asked her to do it," Adal declared. "It's my fault."

Now it was their turn to freeze. They looked at Adal. At her eyes. Then the head manager fired us both: me, for being a worthless C5 girl they could throw away, and Adal for challenging their right to throw me away without consequence. The enforcers would be too reluctant to hurt anyone blessed with moonstone eyes—especially for a lie that everyone knew was a lie. "Get out of here, the rest of you!" the manager growled. The girls pushed for the doors.

In the outside heat, I immediately began to sweat, but my shivering persisted. The other girls, though they knew I was innocent, hurried past me without so much as a glance and dispersed into the alleys leading away from the factories. In the C5 district, fired equaled starvation equaled death. No one wanted to know a dead person.

I stared up at the smogged sky, felt numb, tried to understand how starvation would differ from the persistent hunger I'd felt for years.

"We'll be okay," Adal said, with an impressive amount of confidence.

We could not afford breathers, and so the longer we stayed outside, the more our lungs would burn from the C5 district's polluted air. But fear kept me rooted to the cracked concrete in front of the factory. Adal wrapped her arm around me and pulled me through the damp alleys, swampy with trash. The rare streetlamps revealed bodies in fractions. Here, a bony hand outstretched. Head pillowed on arm, face against concrete. Scraps of gray jumpsuits soiled black. A foot, shoeless, among the trash.

A girl wandered into our path at the end of an alley. She reached for Adal in the flickering orange lamplight. Her eyes were wide and dilated.

"You're here to escort me to the lunar colony?" she asked, voice singsong. Smile haphazard. "Your eyes are like portals! I could step through!"

Adal and I exchanged looks. The girl stumbled forward. Adal caught her. "You're just moondusted," she whispered.

The girl's clothes hung loose on her. She was damp and smelled sour. Where her hair hadn't fallen out from chemical exposure, it was matted and tangled. Adal continued to hold her as if she were a sick friend.

"You'll take me to the moon?" The girl slurred her words, coughed.

"You're moondusted," Adal repeated. "It'll wear off in a couple hours."

I doubted whether the girl had that long to live. Like looking at Sao through a Bliss Viewer, moondust produced an ecstatic high. Unlike the Bliss Viewers, moondust permanently degraded the brain. That, combined with the toxins the girl had been exposed to, meant she was probably incurably sick.

A cough seized me again. We needed to get inside. Adal gave me a look over the girl's shoulder.

"I just want to see the moon," the girl whined.

Adal tried to guide the girl to a seat against a wall. "I'm sorry," she said, letting her go.

The girl's voice, keening, followed us. "I want to go with you! I want to go to the moon!"

The sting of the air grew as my breath quickened. Smog seemed to settle lower, thicker. Muck seeped in through the holes in my shoes. My lungs constricted. Shallow, wheezing breaths. One more block from home and we turned onto a dimly lit street. Skyward lattices of windowless living pods rose on either side of us, their aluminum sides streaked with soot. We'd reach ours soon.

Farther from C5's industrial center, the roads were not paved. In the near-constant rain of summer, the ground became marshy. Every season, news spread of at least one lattice collapse due to unstable foundations. It was late spring.

Satiny blue fabric fluttering out from the shadow of a nearby lattice caught my attention. A silver pockmarked mask turned toward Adal.

I stopped. This was the first time I'd seen one of them. Even in the dim light, the mask gleamed. The robe moved around them as if they were bodiless. Flowers scented the air.

Adal seemed not at all surprised and spared only a furtive glance at the cultist. "Not yet," she whispered. We kept walking. The dark eyeholes in the mask stared after us.

Adal removed her scarf from her hair and tied it over her eyes after we'd climbed up the lattice to our pod. She often did this after work. "Eyestrain," she'd say. "Headache." But tonight she tied the scarf slowly, deliberately, as if her fingers were studying the texture of the fabric.

"It's becoming harder to look at this world," she sighed, settling down on the narrow bunk we shared. "My eyes ... Sometimes I wish I had eyes like yours, Bimi."

"But your eyes are beautiful," I said automatically. My coughs had started to settle down, but my chest and throat were sore from it.

Her lips twitched. "They're too sensitive. Every bad thing I see is magnified."

"But so is every beautiful thing. You get to experience that more strongly than the rest of us."

"Where are beautiful things? Who has beautiful things?" She worried the loose ends of the scarf. "This weighs on me. It's not just objects, it's emotions. Spirit, I think. The managers are dirtier than the streets. And that girl, living in the ruins of herself."

I stood, uncertain, at the door, one of the only spots in the pod where one could stand. The metal ceiling sloped low so that I had to bend my neck and slump my shoulders, and I was starting to feel the ache.

"I want to go somewhere that won't hurt my eyes. Better, a place where they would really feel like a gift."

"Is that what the cultists promised?"

"Yes," said Adal.

"Where have they been taking everyone?"

"To Sao. The A-district citizens can look at the moon, but the cultists have found a way to actually put souls on Sao. I could *be* there."

"How do you know they're telling the truth?"

"I could see. They were the most radiant people. They weren't stained by lies."

"Could they have tricked your sight?" I asked.

"My eyes are true."

I thought about the Bliss Viewer factory girls who had probably been killed for trying to assemble stolen telescope parts, for trying to experience the dopamine high of simply looking at Sao. The moondusted girl dying on the street. I doubted any promises of safety or happiness for girls like us.

Neither of us slept through the night. We alternately held each other, then rolled away, sweating, to opposite sides of the bunk, a couple inches of space between us. We were close, but there was always that last little space between us. In the early hours of the morning, I became restless and got up, searching for anything soothing to occupy my thoughts and hands. All the while, I wished for a splash of cool water on my face.

When I heard Adal stir awake, I asked, "What do they want from you in return?"—because anything involving cultists involved sacrifices.

I stood across from her at the fold-out surface mounted on the wall. The pod was always hot, but today I sweated more than usual, the moisture tickling down my back and soaking into the rough fabric of the jumpsuit. I sweetened the last of our weekly rations of carb powder with sugar from the tin that I hid in the safe under our sleeping bunk. I tried to keep my hands steady as I measured and stirred; I did not want her to see the way emotions were creeping in and making me shake. Adal, quiet, sat up and watched me work in the dim light of our pod's single light bulb. We had no space for chairs, and we couldn't have afforded any even if we had the space, so Adal remained on our bunk.

"What sacrifice?" I repeated.

Adal had nothing valuable to give that I knew of. The pod was too small to hide anything. We both knew about the safe.

"The one I talked to said I was special enough to attain transference."

"Because of your eyes? They'll help you get to Sao somehow?"

She nodded.

I swallowed, my throat dry from lack of water and something else. I glanced down at the brittle paper card as I continued mixing the contents of the antique plastic bowl. The recipe had been passed down in my family from a time when food for common people wasn't wholly reduced to powdered versions of its components, when words were put to paper instead of holofilm. The card of the recipe was frayed at the corners, yellowed. I stored it with the sugar tin, and each rare moment I took it out, it disintegrated a little more. I'd transferred the original recipe along with my experimental ratios for carb and protein powders to holofilm in order to preserve the original, but today I needed to hold the paper.

Cake? Adal had tried the sound when I first attempted the recipe years ago, overemphasizing the hard snaps of the word.

Sweetened carbs held together with moisture and protein, I'd explained. I didn't know if I'd ever get the finished product anywhere close to what my ancestors had eaten, to what I was sure the chancellor and the rest of the A-district people still ate.

"How long will you be gone?" I asked, stirring faster. The ingredients were well combined. My upper arm burned. I could have stopped but didn't.

"Transference lasts forever. My soul will exist on Sao. My body here will be unconscious."

I gripped the bowl of batter too hard when I turned to offer it to her. "Forever?" I repeated.

I had never had anything to heat the mix in order to complete the final step, never had enough water to thin the batter out properly. But this was the most precious thing I had to give.

She took the bowl from me. "My sacrifice will pay the way for two if you want to come. We can live on Sao forever. Happy and safe and together," she said. She spooned a chunk of cake batter onto her fingertips, lifted it to her lips, paused, and plucked a white flower bud from beneath her tongue. She held it on her palm while she licked the batter from her fingers.

Night-blooming, I remembered from the rumors. I wondered if, when the sun set, I might watch it unfurl there in her hand.

"The cultists can smell the flowers," she explained before I could ask. "It's how they'll find me when I'm ready to go with them. When we're ready to go."

The batter was dense and stuck our tongues to the tops of our mouths, and when I could swallow and free my tongue, I said, "You mean we can escape? Like the chancellor and the other A-district people do but forever?"

"Yes!" She took another bite of cake. She pulled her sleeve over her hand to polish her right eye. A nervous habit. Even in the unflattering light of the pod, the cabochons of her eyes glimmered a hard rainbow.

"But the sacrifice," I said. Wouldn't everyone go live in bodiless eternal bliss on Sao if it were that easy? Could anyone really live there if the happiness of just looking at it disorients whoever sees it?

Adal frowned and made a noise around the cake in her mouth. When she could speak again, she said, "You know what happens next if we stay here."

I looked into the bowl of lumpy batter and crunched the undissolved sugar between my teeth. Thought of the fired girls whose gray jumpsuits were soaked black with toxic garbage. Adal cupped my face. Her hands were sticky with sugar. "I'm sorry. I just want you with me."

"What if we could find another job?" I asked.

She sighed and dropped her hands into her lap, cupping the flower. "Just trust me. Come with me."

Two blue-robed lunar cultists pinged our pod near midnight. Like the one I'd seen before, they wore shining silver masks patterned like the surface of a moon, small eye holes set into the shallow craters. Adal handed them two strips of silvery holofilm I hadn't seen before now. They studied them, nodded, and floated to the ground, leaving the scent of clean water and white flowers in their wake. We climbed the lattice down after them.

Adal produced the flower from under her tongue. It had begun to blossom. The cultists nodded and started wordlessly into the night, the deep blue of their robes smears in the darkness. The swirl of wind revealed no feet. The fabric didn't catch against a body as it billowed. Adal looked small and faded next to the cultists.

We passed through the ruins of the old city that C5 was born out of, a grid of skeletal structures lancing the sky. Despite its brokenness, the air here was easier to breathe. The farther out we marched, vines began to twist over the ruins of the city. Then, in the cracked concrete, I spied grass growing all stubborn and wiry. Adal squeezed my hand. I tried to smile at her. The flower in the palm of her other hand glowed harsh and white in the moonlight as the crumbling structures around us gave way to desolate countryside.

On a distant hill, the spherical shadow of a structure stood out against the night. The masks turned to study us. Adal held her flower up to the sky, and its glow washed the deep brown of her face in eerie light that hollowed her features. I wished she had never freed it from under her tongue, never let it bloom. We headed for the shadow.

At the structure, the cultists marched us up a series of stairs until my legs burned and my lungs, weakened from a lifetime of toxic air, constricted. I tripped up several steps, wheezed. They finally listened to Adal when she pleaded for a break. I gasped ineffectually for air until the cool satin of their robes settled around me and buoyed me up the last steps as if I were propelled on a gentle wave.

We emerged into the sphere of an observatory, its domed roof cracked open like the egg of my ancestor's recipes. An abandoned relic of the age before the chancellors took power. In a spot of moonlight at the center of the room, white flowers bloomed.

I'd never seen the sky so clear. Hadn't known there were places where it was still so clear. Clean darkness dotted with crisp silver light.

The cultists let us have our moment with the sky. Adal hugged me and pressed her cheek against mine as we looked up. A breeze whispered through the observatory, brushing crisp air against our faces.

I glanced away from the sky, and my chest seized again. The cultists were not hurrying us because they were making preparations for the transference, moving in a silent sweep of robes.

Two shells of machinery, throne-like in height and strung with cables, dominated the center of the room. The cultists swirled around them as if in a dance, snaking the cables of the shells across the room to another machine in the shadows. When they were done, four of them advanced, a pair beckoning us each toward one of the shells.

They guided us to sit. I could only look at Adal. She seemed too far away. She reached up to rub at her eye. A cultist took her arm and strapped it down.

"Why are you restraining us?" I asked.

No one answered. One of the cultists securing Adal brought down a metal ring that secured her head to the apparatus. I got no such thing.

"Does it hurt?" I asked. "Does it hurt?"

Adal tried to shake her head. "I'm fine," she said, trying to smile for me.

A whirring noise started above us, and two metal arms descended from an unbroken place in the ceiling. They paused in front of Adal's face, the claws at the ends of them clacking, calibrating. The cultist at the block of machinery input a series of commands after conferring with the one who'd strapped Adal in. She tried to turn her face away as the claws moved in, but the metal ring held her. My chest wound tight. The claws came away with Adal's eyes glinting a pale rainbow in their clutches. Adal's face, her beautiful face, hollow. Holes staring out, weeping a trickle of blood. She twisted her mouth, flexed her hands wildly, the only part of her that she could move. She breathed, air rushing in out, in out, so loud I imagined I could feel her breath in my lungs.

My sacrifice will pay the way for two, she'd said.

"Adal? Adal?" I repeated her name. A question, a cry. I struggled uselessly.

Adal tried to reply. Gritted her teeth.

Two cultists stepped forward, each holding a moonstone. An eye. They slotted Adal's eyes into sockets just over our heads.

"You'll return them to her after this? Return her sight?" I questioned.

"The transference chassis—" the cultist in front of me finally spoke, "—is focused by moonstone." Their voice was soft as if they weren't used to speaking, the rhythm of the words off like someone unused to speaking the government-enforced common language. Starlight caught the eyes within the dark holes of the mask as they stared up at the moonstone—the eye—they'd placed above me. Their silvered mask shined too bright, and I squinted, looked away. "The process of connecting to Sao, a strong moon, blesses the stone for later ritual."

"What ritual?" I said. "What do you do with all of them?"

The cultist turned the holes of their mask to meet my gaze. Leaned in and whispered with the girlish delight of sharing a secret. "We will give strength back to the Earth moon."

I was struck by the voice. "You're girls like us?"

"In your language, you'd call us that. But we are stronger. Eternal. And not of Earth." I thought I sensed a smile beneath the mask. "Terrans invade the Earth satellite, our goddess, our moon. She will not become another of your ruins."

"Can't we help you fix it?"

"You have helped," the cultist said. "Now you can rest."

The robed figures wheeled Adal's apparatus beneath the open sky and starlight—"We'll be together soon. On Sao," Adal said—and it was then that I glimpsed the outlines of similar silhouettes along the back wall. Rows and rows of girls, eyeless and dreaming.

Adal's voice was hazy, distant. I saw her stumbling on the cold black horizon, hands out in front of her, two hollows in her face.

"Bimi?" she cried. "Bimi?"

But the ground, so silver and shining. Shifting beneath my feet like powdered diamond. I could look at it forever. Wanted to look at it forever. Couldn't raise my eyes to anything else. Couldn't leave this most perfect spot in the universe. I'd landed here! How lucky to be here and alive! Why did I, of all people, deserve to witness this beauty? This one last beauty?

I fell into the moondust, scooped it up in great handfuls, smeared it across my skin. So beautiful. Forever.

The voice on the horizon was stumbling away, turning off. I think I heard her shriek and fall and get back up again, but really, she should have stayed close to the moon, in its beautiful, beautiful dust.

I was very blissed when a cold foot stepped on my hand. My head was heavy now as if sleep had weight and had been stuffed into my skull. When I managed to turn my neck to look at the foot, I saw it had passed through my hand so that our bodies occupied the same space.

How long had I been staring into the void of sky and sweeping moondust across my body?

Over the pile of shimmering particles on my chest, an eyeless face turned down towards me. This face had a sound that went with it, a tender sound I loved.

"Adal," I said. "Adal." I sat up and left the dust behind.

Her lips trembled into a smile. "I've walked the moon so many times looking for you. It's been—forever."

I stood to embrace her and realized my soul-body was so heavy. Moving took years. Every inch of space, so far. Remember how to raise an arm. Step forward.

But when we touched and melted through each other, I knew her soul, and it was the closest we'd ever been.

FOR WANT OF SISTERHOOD; OR, A POISON GIRL'S FATE

T HE MARSH UNSWALLOWS ME. Escape and desperate flight have found me here, before an immaculate manor house with a sprawling but dead garden. Or a decrepit house with a manicured garden. The landscape ebbs and flows between beauty and decay like this—a dew-speckled rose flourishing in defiance of its withered bush, a crumbling sculpture made whole on second look. I pause before one of many statues of ladies in blush-inducing postures. An ample bosom shelters an abandoned bird's nest. I turn away from another as a palm-sized spider drops from its web between stone breasts. Finally, after a harrowing journey through the autumn mist, I arrive at a gleaming brass handle within a great but rotted door. I knock. Almost immediately, the door opens, as if the house's inhabitant felt me tiptoeing through the garden.

I recoil from the lady's beauty, shrinking into the shadows from whence I came. She can be none other than Lady Borouch, dreaded cultess, enchantress, and—I hope—my savior. She's stunning where I am nothing but bones and angles, a starved thing. Her rich brown skin is dewy in the candlelight from beyond her doorway. For a moment, I am lost in the inky depths of her eyes, too round, too large, shining with grim knowledge. Her braids pool on the marble with skirts of bruised purple lace and smoky silk. The daring cut of her bodice bares her breasts, a style I have only seen on the women attending the orgies I was sometimes tasked with presiding over. (It wouldn't do for someone to poison the wine and spoil the mood.) The first time I was stunned by a lady wearing such style, she'd laughed at me, at my naivety. But the woman before me now doesn't laugh. Her gaze is utterly serious.

"You've traveled far," she says, observing my rain-damp curls, the mud staining the hem of my threadbare gray dress. There's something irregular about her voice. I swear a whisper trails it, echoing the same words.

"I've come to join the sisterhood," I say, drawing my shoulders back, holding my head high. The confidence is unnatural. I hope she doesn't notice.

She smiles pleasantly and without teeth, stepping aside to allow my entry. The manor is pleasantly warm. A chandelier of cut onyx shimmers darkly in the domed entryway. A grand staircase winds up either side of the room, black candles dripping wax upon the banister. At first look, the pattern of the stone floor appears chaotic, black whorls turning to sharp angles and back, all crossing one over the other. Despite their lack of cohesion, they draw the eye inward, ushering one towards the house's bleak depths. Where faded wallpaper has sagged from the walls, lurid green lies beneath. The silence is massive, a weight in the air. I'm still reckoning with the menacing union of grandiosity and disrepair when the lady says, "Please leave your stained clothes at the door."

My attention snaps back to her. She stares at me, waiting expectantly and offering nothing to replace what she's asked me to discard. I don't know if the lady is of noble blood, but she commands like one born to wealth. I strip in front of her, for her, shivering away the last of the marsh's chill. Her gaze is soft, admiring. If she's offended by my ribs, my sharp elbows, she doesn't show it. She beckons me to follow her. The marble floor is icy under my step as we cross the foyer and climb the stairs. She leads me down a maze of gloomy halls to a darker drawing room.

Embers glimmer in the hearth. Heavy velvet curtains banish any moonlight that might've watched over us, and only a scattering of candles light the room. My eyes struggle. I cannot find the ceiling. I stumble over an ottoman as I follow the lady and try not to pin the train of her gown underfoot. Shadowed portraits of owl-eyed women follow our progress through the room. The lady takes up a velvet settee by the fireplace.

"Sit. Please," she says, gesturing to the seat across from her.

Self-conscious, I do as I'm told. Between us, a low table bears a tea spread. I wait to speak as the lady pours ceylon. She serves my tea herself along with a selection of delicate cakes, and my eyes water as I take them from her. People of her station barely spare me a glance, let alone offer me kindness from their own hands. She looms over me as I take my first tentative sips, burning my tongue as tears slip down my cheeks.

"Thank you," I whisper, my throat tight.

She smiles down at me, taking my chin carefully between her fingers. The touch of her gloves is cool against my skin, and I imagine, for a fleeting moment, catching a silk fingertip with my teeth and tugging the fabric free.

"My Lady," I begin, but she silences me with a delicate square of cake to my lips. I accept it and thank her and try to stop crying, but I'm a fool who will do anything for a scrap of tenderness. The cake dissolves on my tongue, a perfect marriage of sugar and butter I've never experienced before. I blink up at her, and she's blurry through my tears.

Seemingly satisfied by my easy undoing, she returns to her place across from me.

Embarrassed, I sniffle and wipe at my eyes, fighting for composure. "Where are the sisters?" I ask, gazing into the gloom. Like the mists of the marsh, the darkness here ensures I can't see far. I wonder at how oppressive it suddenly seems, as if even the scant candles we passed as we entered have gone out.

Lady Borouch smiles into her tea. "You'll meet them soon enough if we decide to take you in." She says it lightly, unthreateningly, but the *if* wedges in my ribs like a knife. "What can you offer the sisterhood?"

Her sharp gaze doesn't miss the way I clench my hands in my lap.

"I don't have any means or talents." I stare into the dark pool of tea. "I was a mere poison girl."

The lady's eyes widen at that, as if I've told her I've mastered three instruments and command five languages. "Then you have a strength and bravery few can claim."

"There were no other options to someone born into my position."

"Yet every day you wake and stare down death to shield another."

Angry tears grip me. "Because I am worthless."

"You are priceless."

Finally, I meet her gaze again. Lady Borouch seems so like those I've served before, and yet she regards me with admiration. "Before admitting girls to the sisterhood, we ask them to demonstrate the talent they offer the collective."

I swallow. "Certainly."

Anguish is often a poison girl's only friend. Or at least that's the way some made peace with their fate, finding a thrill in how our work was a knife point always at our throats. Our purging, though it saved their lives, was often distasteful to the nobles we served. I didn't understand until I witnessed another of us imbibe poison, how she collapsed as if possessed. To purge poison from the system is a great feat requiring a body's complete focus. One cannot be pretty and demure. I didn't want to disturb the lady and endanger her opinion of me.

"Though may I ask," I add tentatively, "if you've ever seen a poison girl at work?"

The lady's lips quirk in amusement. "I assure you nothing disturbs me."

Two claps summon a hollow-eyed girl from the gloom. She moves disjointedly as if on marionette strings. A long fall of dark hair is all she has for modesty. Guilt chases dread. I don't know what was stolen from her to turn her so empty, but the horror of my ignorance and complicity overwhelms me. While I took sweets from the lady's hand, while I entertained a fantasy of kindness, this girl stood alone with nothing.

I'm so alarmed by her manner, by the fact that she'd been lurking in the depths of the room since we entered, that at first I miss the silver tray she bears. On it, a rare white blossom. The sight of it banishes my moral dilemma. My breath catches in my throat, gaze darting from the lady to the flower. I could risk death as I have always done—though almost certainly this time. Even for most poison girls, weeping luna is often fatal. Its scent alone can be deadly, an ozone that reeks of collapse.

But the girl doesn't deliver the tray to me. She kneels before Lady Borouch, so intimately close it raises heat to my cheeks despite my pounding heart. The lady thanks the girl with a mystifyingly chaste kiss and takes the flower between thumb and forefinger, leaning back easily on her settee as if with nothing more than a glass of red wine. The girl, unmoved by the kiss, retreats to the shadows.

I'm on my feet, about to warn of all the properties of weeping luna, when the lady plucks a petal free and places it on her tongue like a sacrament. She rests her arms upon the back of the seat and levels her gaze on me as if this is nothing more than a flirtatious dare. "If you want to join the sisterhood, you must first save it."

I trip over the leg of the table and fall at her feet. Her gaze turns hungry, rapt. She plucks another petal and presses it to my lips, a dark parody of our earlier exchange. Trembling, I accept it obediently.

Bitter acidity blooms in my mouth. I gag on the taste, but the lady braces me, holding my face in her hands. I swallow, and she smiles as the poison burns down my throat.

"My lady—" I rasp, knowing that she only has minutes, perhaps seconds, before the poison takes her.

She silences my concern with a fierce kiss, and despite the first involuntary twist of the purge, she holds me steady. Her tongue finds mine, and I am certain we'll both meet our ends here, tangled in the grip of death and pleasure.

Drawing poison after it's entered another's body is the hardest part of our work. We are scrupulous in tasting food and drink before others partake precisely because locating and subduing poison within another is harder than purging it from oneself. Now, I must do both at once—against the toxicity of weeping luna.

I choose the lady first and am thankful for her firm and grounding touch. My consciousness longs to slip beneath the waves as my body undertakes its work, but I must stay awake. For her, for this cursed sisterhood.

I map the contours of the lady's inner landscape, the complex web of her veins, the slick tissues between them. I'm entranced by the red pulp and viscera of her. It's beautiful here, nestled in the quickening beat of her flesh. We're an ouroboros of ecstasy, endangered by our own hunger. I disentangle myself enough to look deeper, to save us. After years of unfortunate practice, it takes only a moment. The rest is intuitive. There is *her*. There is *not-her*, the poison. I chart its path backwards, unwinding its fatal spread. I am only vaguely aware of my own body or even of hers. Yet here I am within her. The contradiction turns at the edge of my struggling thoughts.

Her. Not-her. The simple divide fractures. Not-her multiplies as I stretch my awareness deeper. I'm startled by the irregular spread of the poison, how it's defied predictable progression through blood and tissue—until I realize it's not poison. The not-her includes *others*. Weeping, screaming, howling others. The sisters of an absent sisterhood. The spirits of other hollow-eyed girls.

I fall back from their screams and into my body, finding myself still snared in the lady's kiss. Dizzily, I register the mess of half discarded lace and silk, the air perfumed with the earthy damp of arousal. I'm astride her bare thigh. Swollen, wet. Her nails dig into my hips.

I understand the other poison girls now, what it means to merge into another and know them so intimately, more than they could ever know themselves. I understand the ecstasy of the purge, the dangerous pull for more.

The lady rests her forehead against my breastbone as if suddenly weary. The poison. Spreading despite my efforts.

"Save me," she gasps, looking up into my eyes. "You're the only one who can redeem me."

"The sisterhood," I stammer. "You've trapped them. You're—"

She grasps my shoulders and pushes me off her, pinning me to the settee. Her nails didn't seem so sharp before, but now they dig into me like talons. She looms again, her long hair curtaining the room away.

"Judge me, then. What am I? A thief? A liar? What would you have me do with such a lonely heart?" She swoons, her eyes glazed. "I promise you I had but the purest intention. Will you join our sisterhood, save it?"

Reality melts as the poison begins to numb my senses. The dull colors of the room run like bleeding paints. Time presses down on this moment, stretching it like a delicate confection. The lady grinds into me, this game of ruinous possibility—her powerlessness—urging her forward.

No one has ever pleaded for me to save them. Commanded, yes, but commands are not vulnerable. At best, a good poison girl is treated like a prized horse, a breathing object kept for a purpose. One does not ask the horse if she fancies the bit or the punishing journey that follows. When our uncanny insight and natural resistances are discovered, we're taken from our homes and gifted to dignitaries and nobles, a first line of defense against the most subtle assassination attempts. Many nobles will go through several poison girls, but I grew strong. I ingested what should have killed me many times over, and against the odds, I survived.

I choose to save the lady because I can. I save her for all the spirits she houses, one small act for a multitude of girls as desperate as me.

"Yes," I gasp against her mouth, to the languid thrust of her fingers inside me. I clench around her, let the poison flood my veins. When the convulsions seize me, I can't untangle if I'm meeting death or rapture, yet I moan with the chorus of spirits—all of us wounded, ruined treasures raising a collective howl.

Acknowledgments

A heartfelt thank you to all the editors who originally accepted these pieces for publication.

"A Serpent for Each Year" appeared in *Strange Horizons*

"Not Death nor the Storm" appeared in the Neon Hemlock anthology *Unfettered Hexes: Queer Tales of Insatiable Darkness*

"Despair, Divided" appeared in Neon Hemlock's *Baffling Magazine*

"In Case You're the One to Devour a Star" appeared in *Beneath Ceaseless Skies*

"When You Find a Dragon, Name Them for Me" appeared in *Fiyah*

"On Lore" appeared in *Fireside Magazine*

"In Our Season" appeared in the Dark Moon Books anthology *Professor Charlatan Bardot's Travel Anthology to the Most (Fictional) Haunted Buildings in the Weird, Wild World*

"The Future in Salt Water" appeared in *Anathema: Spec from the Margins* and was anthologized in *The Year's Best African Science Fiction: Volume One*

"At the Mouth of the Sea" appeared in *Mermaids Monthly*

"A Vision of Moonlight" was originally published as "Our Souls to the Moon" in *Strange Horizons*

About the Author

Tamara Jerée's short stories have appeared in the Shirley Jackson Award-winning anthologies *Unfettered Hexes: Queer Tales of Insatiable Darkness* and *Professor Charlatan Bardot's Travel Anthology*. Their poem "goddess in forced repose" in *Uncanny Magazine* was nominated for the inaugural Ignyte Award. They've worked as a writer in the video games industry and as an indie bookseller.

instagram.com/tamarajeree

twitter.com/TamaraJeree

www.tamarajeree.com